Eve stiffened,  him she was re

"Okay," she said with chin. "Then tell me

His blue eyes warming affectionately, he was equal to her challenge. "I think Christmas is a magical time of year."

"Because?" Eve prodded.

"The holiday opens up people's hearts and brings them together in ways they often aren't the rest of the year." Derek paused and gave her another long, telling look. "Christmas makes all things seem possible."

It was certainly making this seem possible, Eve thought, aware she barely knew him and already she felt as if they were a couple. Eve studied him right back. "You really are romantic, deep down."

To her satisfaction, he did not even try to deny it.

"What does Christmas mean to you?" he continued.

He'd been remarkably honest. Eve knew she should be, too. Struggling to put her feelings into words, she raked her teeth across her lower lip. "I think it's great if you have a big happy family, like you apparently do."

Once again, he seemed to intuit all she wasn't saying. "But otherwise?" Derek tucked a strand of hair behind her ear.

Eve appreciated the tender feeling of his fingers against her skin. "It can be—it has been—the loneliest time of the year for me."

Derek smiled and dropped his hand. "Then it's time that changed."

...was still too unsure just how close to
him she was ready to be.

Dear Reader,

The holidays are an emotional time of year. For some of us, deeply so. Eve Loughlin has never experienced the true joy of Christmas. She has accepted that for her, and her family, this is just the way it is. Yet she still feels a pang when December rolls around and she sees the giddy excitement of those around her.

Derek McCabe grew up with all the advantages. For him, Christmas was a time when family abounded and dreams came true. Yet now, as a divorced dad, he worries he will not be able to provide his baby girl with the same happiness he experienced.

Eve is ready to help Derek find the perfect home in which to raise his daughter. She doesn't expect, however, in this season of miracles, to find such bliss of her own. And when she does, she can't help but wonder if such unexpected happiness will last.

I hope you enjoy reading this story as much as I enjoyed writing it. For more information on this and other titles, please visit me on Facebook and at www.cathygillenthacker.com.

Happy holidays,

Cathy Gillen Thacker

THE TEXAS CHRISTMAS GIFT

—

CATHY GILLEN THACKER

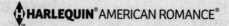

HARLEQUIN® AMERICAN ROMANCE®

Recycling programs
for this product may
not exist in your area.

ISBN-13: 978-0-373-75481-6

THE TEXAS CHRISTMAS GIFT

Copyright © 2013 by Cathy Gillen Thacker

Printed in U.S.A.

ABOUT THE AUTHOR

Cathy Gillen Thacker is married and a mother of three. She and her husband spent eighteen years in Texas and now reside in North Carolina. Her mysteries, romantic comedies and heartwarming family stories have made numerous appearances on bestseller lists, but her best reward, she says, is knowing one of her books made someone's day a little brighter. A popular Harlequin author for many years, she loves telling passionate stories with happy endings, and thinks nothing beats a good romance and a hot cup of tea! You can visit Cathy's website at www.cathygillenthacker.com for more information on her upcoming and previously published books, recipes and a list of her favorite things.

Books by Cathy Gillen Thacker

HARLEQUIN AMERICAN ROMANCE

This book is dedicated to Grant James Thacker, the best little brother two sisters could ever have.

Chapter One

"Derek McCabe is *still* on the phone?" the office manager asked.

In *her* private office, no less. Doing her best to curtail her irritation, Eve Loughlin smiled. "Yep."

Sasha handed her a beautiful red poinsettia from a grateful client. "Well, at least he's easy on the eyes."

Worse, Eve thought, hazarding a glance through the glass door, the amazingly successful venture capitalist had to know it. With his dark brown hair, ruggedly chiseled face and mesmerizing blue eyes, he was handsome enough to stop traffic. His broad-shouldered, six-foot-three-inch frame, currently garbed in an elegant, dark gray suit, made him even more of a catch. *If* she'd been looking. She wasn't.

Luckily, at that moment his call ended.

Taking a deep, calming breath, Eve squared her shoulders and walked back into her office.

"Sorry about that," Derek said. "I'm investing in a technology company. There were some last-minute details to work out."

"I understand," Eve replied. Even though she didn't. Why did Loughlin Realty's well-heeled clients think *their* time was somehow more valuable than the agents they employed to buy and sell their houses?

She set the plant on her credenza, next to several other gift baskets and a ribbon-wrapped bottle of champagne, then returned to her desk. "So back to where we were," she continued crisply. Which hadn't been far, given the fact that Derek had taken the call on his cell thirty seconds after he had walked in. "Have you had time to answer the questionnaire I emailed you?"

He shook his head and lowered himself into a chair in front of her desk. "We don't need to bother with that."

Of course they didn't, Eve thought with mounting frustration. She settled into her ergonomically designed swivel chair.

"I know exactly what I'm looking for," he stated amiably.

Eve picked up her notepad and pen. "Then suppose you tell me."

"I want a home in Highland Park, preferably on or near Crescent Avenue. I'd like to pay between seven and eight million for it. It must have at least three bedrooms and two baths. There'll be no need for bank financing, as I plan to pay cash." He paused, allowing her to catch up. "I'd also like to close next week and take possession immediately."

Eve finished writing and looked into the most gorgeous eyes she had ever seen. "I gather this is just an investment?"

"Much more, actually." His sensual lips lifted into an easy grin. "I plan to live there with my daughter." Affection laced his low voice. "So if you could just find something and let me know…" He glanced at his phone again, which was chiming quietly, then rose as if to leave.

Eve stood and moved around her desk. Because of

the eight-inch difference in their heights, which was modified only slightly by her three-inch heels, she had to tilt her head to look up at him. "When will you be available to look at properties?" she asked, knowing from experience that he was going to be one of those demanding clients who didn't want to waste an instant.

Derek grimaced. He shoved back the edges of his suit jacket, the impatient action briefly diverting her gaze to his flat abs and lean hips. "I only want to look at one."

Lifting her chin, Eve studied him for a long beat. She couldn't help wondering if the sexy venture capitalist was this way with everyone he hired. Or just the nonessential personnel? "You expect me to choose your home?" she asked drily.

He glanced at his watch as his phone chimed again, his deep blue eyes narrowing. "Yes."

Wanting to make this work—but only to a point— Eve held up a palm. "Then I'm going to need a lot more information."

Derek frowned. He might be only thirty-four, if the information she had found on Google prior to meeting him was correct, but he was all autocratic executive. "I'm too busy for that right now."

Which left her no choice. She walked him to the door and opened it wide. "Then," she said, just as imperiously, not about to make herself miserable—especially at this time of year—by working with a man who was far too big for his britches, "you'll have to find yourself another Realtor."

Derek stared in amazement. "You're firing me as a client?"

Eve nodded and ushered him out. Then she smiled one last time. "Consider it my Christmas present to myself."

Two HOURS LATER, as she entered the conference room for the Friday afternoon staff meeting, Eve was still trying to figure out how to tell her mother what she'd done.

The two other sales agents, Vanessa and Astrid, were already there. Eve's mom—the owner of the company—was seated at the head of the table. As always, Marjorie Loughlin was beautifully dressed, today in a red wool suit and heels, her short silvery-blond hair perfectly coiffed. Despite the artful application of makeup, Eve couldn't help but notice her mother looked tired. But maybe that was to be expected. Like the rest of the staff of the all-female realty firm she had founded, Marjorie put in long hours.

"I have great news," she said. "We are still ahead of Sibley & Smith Realty in annual sales by several million dollars." She paused and massaged her left shoulder. "And you all know what that means."

"More exclusive, top-dollar listings and sales," Astrid declared, already pulling out her calculator.

Vanessa winked. "Not to mention that new Mercedes convertible I've been coveting."

Marjorie dabbed a bead of sweat from her hairline. "Luckily, we all have clients wanting to close on homes before the end of the year." Briefly, she went over the list of Astrid's and Vanessa's clients, as well as her own. Then she turned to Eve, addressing the properties and clients of primary concern. "There's Flash Lefleur's condo—which we really need to get sold before the listing expires—and Derek McCabe."

"Right." Eve steeled herself for her mother's disapproval as she prepared to talk about the latter. "About that…"

Marjorie's hand went to the left side of her neck. "Don't tell me there's a problem there."

Except for the fact I fired him? Not a one.

Eve noted her mother was pressing her hand against the bottom of her jaw. "Mom, are you all right...?"

Marjorie winced, as if in pain.

Something was wrong! Eve rushed toward her in alarm. "Mom!"

Her skin a peculiar ashen gray, Marjorie swayed slightly. "I feel a little dizzy," she said, then slumped in her chair in a dead faint.

ONE HARROWING AMBULANCE ride, admission to the hospital and balloon angioplasty later, Marjorie was finally declared stable and moved to a room in the cardiac care unit. Once she was settled, the doctor came in to go over the results of all the tests, as well as the emergency surgical procedure. "You were lucky. It was only a mild heart attack," the cardiologist announced.

"Impossible," Marjorie declared, still looking awfully pale and anxious, despite the medicines they had given her to help her relax. "I'm in perfect health. It was indigestion. A lunch gone wrong. That was all."

The doctor turned to Eve. "Is your mother always this difficult?"

"Yes," she said.

"No," Marjorie stated at the same moment.

Dr. Jackson smiled and shook his head in silent remonstration, obviously having dealt with similar situations before. He turned back to his patient. "We're going to keep you in the hospital, as a precaution, for forty-eight hours, Mrs. Loughlin. After that, I'd like you to go to the cardiac rehab unit, in the annex across the street, for another month, for further evaluation and treatment."

"That's impossible!" Marjorie folded her arms belligerently. "I have *work* to do."

Clearly unintimidated, the physician countered, "It's absolutely necessary, Mrs. Loughlin. You need to rest and rebuild your strength, and above all else, rethink how you've been living your life."

Marjorie sent Eve a look, begging her to intervene.

"I agree with the doctor," Eve said as the physician slipped from the room, wisely leaving the persuasion to a family member.

"But the annual sales award…"

"I'll see we still get it," Eve promised gently.

Still, Marjorie fretted. "I have a new client, that Houston oilman, Red Bloom, coming in soon to see the Santiago Florres–designed home."

Eve smiled. "Not to worry, Mom. I'll take care of that, too."

"You have Derek McCabe…."

Eve had had plenty of time to regret her foolhardiness. "I'll handle his sale, too," she reassured her mother. *At least I hope I will.*

"You're sure?" Marjorie started to relax, as the meds finally kicked in.

She nodded. Her mother had done so much for her over the years. It was now her turn to be the caretaker. "Just rest now." She bent and kissed Marjorie's temple. And then, hoping like hell it wasn't too late to undo the damage, Eve went to make good on her vow.

"WHAT DO YOU mean, it didn't work out?" Derek's ex-wife said over the phone late the next afternoon. "Marjorie Loughlin is the best Realtor in Dallas!"

"I didn't get her. I was assigned her daughter."

Carleen paused. The sounds of their infant daughter and Carleen's lively household could be heard in the background. "I haven't met Eve Loughlin, but she's supposed to be good, too."

She was beautiful, Derek mused, that was for sure. Temperamental, too. A knock sounded at his door. Aware that his assistant had already left for the day, he said, "Can you hang on a minute?" He walked across his private office and opened the door.

On the other side was the show-stopping beauty who had sent him packing. In a long cashmere coat, vibrant blue business suit and suede heels, Eve Loughlin was the epitome of Texas elegance and style. Around five feet seven inches tall, she was slender and lithe, with great legs and even more spectacular curves. From her full breasts to her narrow waist and hips, there wasn't an inch of her left wanting. And despite his irritation with her, his attraction didn't end there. Her skin was fair and utterly flawless, her nose pert, her cheekbones high and sculpted. Her shoulder-length golden-brown hair was so lush and thick he wanted to sink his hands into it. Most mesmerizing of all, though, were her intelligent, wide-set amber eyes, which seemed to hide as much as they revealed.

Derek swallowed around the sudden dryness of his throat, and tore his eyes from her plump, kissable lips. No good could come of this. "Listen, Carleen, I've got to go."

As always, his ex understood. "I'll see you at five-thirty. Craig and I will have Tiffany ready to go."

"Thanks. See you then." Derek ended the call.

Meanwhile, Eve Loughlin waited with a patient, angelic smile.

Not about to make it easy on her, after the way she

had summarily dismissed him the afternoon before, Derek lifted a brow. Waited.

Her smile only became more cordial and determined. "I'm sorry to interrupt."

If that was the case, Derek thought, she already would have left. "What brings you here?"

"I wanted to apologize for what happened yesterday."

She looked as if she actually might be regretting her actions, if the shadows beneath her eyes—shadows that hadn't been there the day before—were any indication. Derek's attitude softened just a little, even as the rest of him remained wary as all get-out. "I'm listening."

She held her red crocodile briefcase in front of her like a shield. "If you can find it in your heart to forgive me, I'd like to retain your business for Loughlin Realty."

Maybe it was the way his marriage had turned out, or the experiences he'd suffered through with women he had dated since, but he'd had enough fickle women to last him a lifetime. Regarding her skeptically, Derek lounged against his desk, his arms folded. "If that's the case, then why did you fire me as a client in the first place?"

TIME TO GROVEL, Eve thought, setting her briefcase on the seat of the armchair beside her. Not her favorite thing, but in this case, extremely necessary if she was to make good on her promise to her mother. Eve noted the spacious office matched him well. Done in varying shades of gray, with large masculine furniture befitting a man of his physical stature, the executive suite had a beautiful view of downtown Dallas.

Gathering her courage, she looked into Derek Mc-Cabe's vivid blue eyes. "Let's just say it was an all-around bad day." Bad time of year, actually. Christmas always made her feel out of sync and vaguely depressed. "I took my frustrations out on you," she admitted, "and that was definitely not the right thing to do." She lifted her palms apologetically. "I wasn't brought up that way, and as a real estate agent, I certainly wasn't trained to behave like that."

Derek looked her up and down, then paused, his broad shoulders relaxing slightly. "I wasn't brought up that way, either." An awkward silence ensued, and then he slid her a long, thoughtful look. "I probably shouldn't have kept you waiting outside your office for a good half hour while I handled other calls."

Understanding flowed between them, as tangible as their previous frustration. Eve easily met him halfway. "Thanks for acknowledging that."

His eyes twinkled. "So maybe we were both at fault yesterday?"

"Maybe." And there it was, she thought as his rueful smile broadened, the legendary McCabe charm.

"Well, good." He came forward and briefly shook her hand to seal the truce. "Then we have something in common."

Eve's skin tingled as they broke contact and politely stepped away from each other. He inclined his head. "So what's next?" he murmured.

She drew a deep, bolstering breath, then took a seat in the armchair and opened her briefcase. "I'm ready to meet your demands."

His phone chimed. He peered down at it, then set it aside. His full attention on Eve once again, he asked, "What stopped you yesterday?"

Watching him take a seat behind his desk, Eve sensed sugarcoating the situation would get her nowhere with the accomplished businessman. "I didn't want to proceed because I felt selecting a property for you, without knowing anything about you or your specific needs, would be a disservice to us both."

He pressed his fingertips together. "In what way?"

"If you end up purchasing a home you're unhappy with, that dissatisfaction will eventually be heaped on Loughlin Realty. And more specifically, me." Hesitating for a moment, Eve crossed her legs and discreetly tugged her skirt a little lower over her knees. "My reputation depends on being able to find the exact right home for my clients. If I can't do that, I may as well not continue as an agent."

His dark brows furrowed. "That's why you wanted me to fill out the forms?"

Finally, they were getting somewhere! "I don't even know how old your daughter is. Or if she lives with you full-time or part-time, or simply visits."

"Tiffany lives with me fifty percent of the time. My ex and I share custody."

"Do you want her to go to public or private school?"

"Probably public, if we're in the Highland Park district, but we're not there yet. She's just turned one."

What was it about this man that had Eve losing her equilibrium? Usually, she was much better at maintaining a casual, inscrutable demeanor. Blowing out a breath, she attempted to rein in her reaction. "You must be very recently divorced."

"It was final last summer. We were separated for a year and a half before that," he related mildly.

And his child was one now, Eve thought, doing some quick calculations.

"AREN'T YOU GOING to say it?" Derek asked, something akin to disappointment on his handsome face. He studied her bluntly. "What a terrible person I must have been to have left a pregnant wife?"

This felt like some kind of a test. Deliberately, she held his gaze. "I'm sure you had your reasons." Her manner matter-of-fact, she continued, "In any case, it's none of my business."

He appeared to be mulling that over. "So when did you want to get started?" he finally said, after a long, awkward pause.

Glad he had decided to use their firm for his home search, after all, Eve smiled. "I'm available anytime."

"Right now?"

Another test. Eve inhaled and smiled again. "Absolutely."

Derek stood and reached for his coat, all McCabe determination once again. "Then let's go."

Chapter Two

"Mind if I drive?" Derek said as they walked out the door of his swanky office complex.

Whatever the client wanted. Within reason. That was the rule. "Not at all," Eve fibbed. "Where are we going?"

"I have to pick up my daughter by five-thirty. I'll have her until tomorrow evening." He paused to help Eve with her coat, and then escorted her out to a late-model Jaguar SUV. He opened the passenger door, waited for her to slide in, then circled around to the driver's side.

Impressed with his good manners—it had been a long time since she had met anyone so naturally chivalrous—Eve pulled out her notebook again. Determined to keep things strictly business, she asked, "You want to take her with us when we look?"

"Tomorrow, when we go see the house we select, yes. As for this evening, I plan to take her back to my hotel, feed and bathe her, and then put her to bed."

Eve wasn't sure where that left her and the business she needed to conduct.

Derek continued, "And while I do all that, we'll have a little chat about what property would be best suited for my daughter and me."

Eve wasn't surprised. Most single parents were adept multitaskers. Still, she would have preferred they talk under less intimate circumstances. She wanted to know only enough about him and his life to do her job well. Anything else would be just too personal.

He turned onto Crescent Avenue. "I assume you have most of the property specs on the computer?"

Eve nodded. "Including visual tours."

"Then we should be able to pick one."

Derek parked in the driveway of one of the largest, most elegant properties in Highland Park. "Mind giving me a hand? There's a lot of stuff when we switch back and forth."

So now she was a bellboy, too. What next? A nanny? Tamping down her irritation, Eve flashed a smile. "No problem."

This time, she managed to exit the sedan before Derek could gallantly lend a hand. If he noticed her effort to keep things on an impersonal level, he didn't show it. Instead, he seemed distracted, almost eager, as they walked to the front door. The doorbell was answered by an attractive brunette in a silk shirt, heels and jeans. She had a pair of reading glasses perched on the end of her nose and a pen tucked into the short, sophisticated curls above her ear. Her expression was intellectual—and kind.

"Hey, stranger!" She greeted Derek with a friendly pat on the arm and a peck on his cheek. "How's the house-hunting going?"

Derek inclined his head at Eve. "We haven't really started yet. Carleen, this is Eve Loughlin. Eve, Carleen Walton, my ex-wife."

The woman grinned and extended her hand. "It's nice to meet you," she said.

They certainly were friendly, Eve noted. Maybe the most amiable exes she had ever seen. "Nice to meet you, too," she replied.

A tall forty-something man ambled up with a baby in his arms.

"And this is Craig, my husband," Carleen continued. "With our baby, Tiffany."

And what a beautiful baby she was, Eve could not help but note.

The one-year-old had a cloud of dark curly hair, like her mom's, and Derek's vivid sea-blue eyes. She was dressed in a white turtleneck, ruffled red velvet overalls and shiny, high-topped shoes. Spying Eve, she beamed, her smile revealing four teeth, two on the bottom and two on top.

Eve had never been much of a baby person. She saw no reason to lust after something she likely would never have. But something about this little girl captivated her attention.

Still grinning, Tiffany lifted her chubby little hands to her face and spread her fingertips over her eyes. "Peek—boo!" she chirped to Eve.

Eve couldn't help it; she chuckled. She lifted her hands to her own eyes and covered them playfully. "Peekaboo to you, too!"

Tiffany threw back her head and chortled. Without warning, she lurched out of Craig's arms and reached for Eve.

Eve caught the infant, cuddling her close. It wasn't the first time she had ever held a baby. However, it *was* the first time she'd held one and felt something catch in her heart.

"She's a real people person," Carleen noted proudly.

Craig agreed. "Never met a stranger..." he teased.

Tiffany settled in Eve's arms. She had that wonderful baby-fresh scent. A smear of what looked like strawberry yogurt at the corner of her mouth. More of it on her hands.

Tiffany tilted her head to one side. She looked at Eve. "Mommy?" she asked.

"No, I'm not a momma," Eve said.

Although for the first time in her life, she found herself wanting to be.

Behind Craig came half a dozen more kids, from toddlers to teens. One of them was holding a wet baby wipe.

"And the rest of our brood," Craig continued. Catching Eve's confused look, he said, "From my marriage to my late wife."

They all certainly looked happy, Eve thought, like the ideal blended family.

Craig took the wipe and handed it to Eve as more introductions were made.

Too late. The little girl's sticky fingers had found their way to Eve's hair and were wrapped in the long, silky strands, transferring strawberry yogurt even as they tugged.

Tiffany giggled.

Derek jumped in. "Honey, you can't do that," he chided, working to free the tiny fingers.

"It's okay," Eve said.

And despite the stickiness, she really didn't mind.

The close contact had given her a glimpse into the little girl's personality. And what was there was all sweetness and innocence.

She could see why Derek was so bent on being as close to his daughter as he could. And she admired the friendship and cooperation his ex and her new family demonstrated, as Carleen put a hat and jacket on their little girl before Derek took charge of putting Tiffany into her car seat. Craig and the kids carried several large bags of clothes and toys, and a stroller, out to the car.

"I hope you can find something for Derek without too much delay," Carleen told Eve pleasantly.

Craig nodded. "Life will be a lot easier for them when they're in a house instead of a hotel."

Where was the acrimony that usually existed in recently divorced couples? Eve wondered. Not that there was a residual attraction between them, either. The only love Carleen and Derek seemed to harbor for each other was the old-and-trusted-friends variety. Although why that would be a relief to Eve, she didn't know. She was just helping Derek buy a house, not becoming part of this unorthodox situation.

Eve returned Carleen's and Craig's smiles. She dipped her head in acquiescence, promising, "I'll do my very best."

"ANYONE EVER TELL you that you have the patience of a saint?" Derek asked several hours later, as he paced the length of his two-bedroom hotel suite, his drowsy daughter in his arms.

He had shed the suit and tie shortly after they'd walked in, emerging from the bedroom in a pair of worn jeans and the same pale blue dress shirt he'd had on earlier. With the first two buttons undone, sleeves rolled to just below the elbow and the hem untucked, he looked casual and at ease. Having gotten a glimpse of the man he was in his off hours, Eve liked what she saw. It also gave her hope that she would eventually be able to connect with him on a more congenial level, and talk some sense into him when it came to looking for a place to call home.

In the meanwhile, Tiffany had resisted being tucked in, so Derek was now "walking" her to sleep. It seemed to be working, Eve noted, as she watched the little girl lay her head on his broad shoulder and slowly close her eyes.

Eve smiled as Tiffany yawned again and cuddled even closer against her daddy's big strong frame. Eve sighed despite herself. Was there anything more compelling than watching a man tenderly care for a child?

Abruptly aware that Derek was watching her as intently as she was watching him, Eve brushed aside the fantasies he'd been engendering all evening and reassured him with a smile. "Not to worry. Adjusting my schedule to my client's is a necessary component of my vocation."

She hadn't planned to be there through Tiffany's dinner and bath, but it had given her time to get better acquainted with Derek and his daughter and intermittently ask him questions about what he wanted in a home. Which in turn gave her a better idea what properties to show him.

Noting his daughter was now sound asleep, Derek carried her into the adjacent bedroom and set her ever so gently down in her crib. He paused to cover her with a blanket, and then returned to the living room. With his dark hair attractively mussed, the hint of evening beard rimming his handsome face and his long legs emphasized by close-fitting jeans, he was the epitome of masculinity. And *way* too sexy for her own good, Eve reminded herself.

He plucked the bottle of sparkling water from the

room service tray, filled two glasses and added ice, then handed her one. "Ready to get down to business?"

She accepted the beverage with a smile. "Let's do it."

She brought up the map of Highland Park on her computer. The town was three miles north of the center of Dallas, and only 2.26 square miles in size. Yet it had approximately 8,900 residents, most living in very luxurious and expensive homes. "Exactly how close do you want to be to your ex-wife's place?"

Shrugging in response, he pulled up a chair beside her at the desk. He turned it around and sank onto it, his long limbs on either side of the seat, his arms folded over the back. After a moment of deliberation, he slanted Eve a glance. "Next door wouldn't be bad."

She turned toward him so abruptly her stocking-clad knee brushed his denim-clad thigh. A flicker of sensation swept through her. "Seriously?"

He lifted his shoulders in another shrug. "Just because Carleen and I are divorced doesn't mean we can't give Tiffany the same level of familial happiness she would have enjoyed had we stayed together." He studied Eve over the rim of his glass. "You don't believe that can happen?"

She paused, not sure how to answer that. "You two seem to get along great."

Her caution made him smile and search her eyes. "And you think that's weird."

Eve wanted to deny it. But she sensed if she was less than honest, she would lose him as a client. She shifted so they were no longer in danger of touching, and leaned back in her seat. "I think it's commendable."

He waited, still studying her.

Eve gulped some water, aware she was going to have to open up even more. "And…unusual," she said finally.

She lowered her eyes to the strong column of his throat and the tufts of springy, dark brown hair beneath his collarbone, then quickly looked back up. Clearing her throat, Eve tried for diplomacy. "I'm not married. Never have been. But from what I've seen, sharing custody can be really challenging."

He lifted a brow. "You mean ugly."

"Or just plain difficult." She shrugged, still feeling as if she were walking through a minefield, courtesy of Derek McCabe. "Given that there are so many emotions involved in these kinds of situations..."

His gaze drifted over her face slowly, before returning to her eyes. "You're wondering why I'm okay with my wife remarrying."

Was she that easy to read? And why did she, a consummate professional who made a point these days to keep her personal feelings out of every business situation, really want to know? Telling herself it would help her find the right home for him if she knew more about the overall situation, she shifted a little closer. "Are you?"

He nodded, then rose and walked back to the room service table where several desserts sat untouched. He picked up a plate and gestured for her to have at it, too. "Maybe if Carleen and I had been head over heels in love, I'd feel differently."

He'd chosen the slice of coconut cake garnished with berries. Eve picked up the crème brûlée.

He settled himself on the sofa. She selected an adjacent wingback chair and spread a napkin over her lap. "But you weren't in love?" This was getting more interesting by the moment.

Derek exhaled, regret sharpening his handsome features. "We were really great friends from the moment we met at Harvard Business School. We both worked in the financial sector, and wanted the same things, including high-powered careers—and kids. And we figured if you were going to have a family, you should be married."

"So you tied the knot."

Savoring another bite of cake, he nodded. "For the first couple of years it was great. We moved back to Texas, where our families were from. We had work and each other. And then Carleen and I met Craig. One of Carleen's coworkers, he had recently lost his wife to cancer. Needless to say, our hearts went out to him. We started helping him with his brood of kids whenever we could. But I was traveling a lot with my job then, so Carleen spent more time over there." There was a long silence. "The experience made her really want children, so we started working on a family of our own. She had just found out she was pregnant when I walked in one day and saw the way they looked at each other."

Eve's heart stilled. She paused, her spoon halfway through the sugary crust on her crème brûlée. "They were having an affair?" She couldn't fathom that, remembering the two people she'd met earlier.

Putting his empty plate aside, Derek exhaled roughly and clamped a hand to the back of his neck. "No, they were both too principled for that. But it was clear to me that Carleen was in love with Craig, the way she never had been with me." He paused, rubbing the tense muscles.

Eve watched Derek rummage around for a coffee cup. Finding one, he filled it from the decanter on the room service tray. "You must have been devastated," she said.

The look on his face said he had been. "I thought

about ignoring it," he confided quietly, coming back to sit on the sofa. "Just hoping and praying whatever it was they were obviously feeling would fade."

Eve remembered that they had separated early in Carleen's pregnancy. "But you didn't do that."

He shrugged and turned his eyes back to hers, a mixture of remorse and acceptance visible there. "I realized I couldn't live a lie for the rest of my life. So I asked Carleen about it, and she finally admitted what I had already observed. That, in an ideal world, she probably *would* have ended up with Craig…but she was married to me, and she intended to *stay* married to me."

"You disagreed?"

He gestured with a weariness that seemed to come from deep in his soul. "Pretending feelings don't exist doesn't mean they aren't there. I wanted Carleen to be happy. And I knew she belonged with Craig."

That was gallant. But… "You weren't the least bit jealous?"

He rubbed his jaw in a rueful manner, then drawled, "Let's just say I wanted what they were having for myself."

That made sense, Eve thought. Everyone was entitled to the love of a lifetime. Whether or not a person ever actually achieved that was a different matter entirely.

"So, the two of us split up," Derek continued. "I stayed involved with the pregnancy and was there for the birth. For propriety's sake, we waited to finalize our divorce until Tiffany was six months old. A short engagement followed. And then Craig and Carleen got married in late October and relocated from Houston to Dallas—so that Carleen could have a job with greater flexibility. I made arrangements to follow suit."

Eve studied the attractive man sitting opposite her.

He really was one of the most honorable men she had ever met. But she couldn't help but wonder if all that selflessness came with a price.

DEREK WASN'T SURE why he was talking about any of this. He certainly didn't need to tell Eve about his broken marriage in order for her to find him a suitable home. And yet there was something about the way she looked at him, as if she wanted to understand—not just the situation, but get to know him in a way few did— that had started him talking, and kept him talking when he should have stopped.

"This is the point where you tell me I should have made the most of my ex's foibles and fought for full custody of my kid," he said cavalierly, wanting to see her gut reaction to his situation. To find out if she was as skeptical and disapproving as his family and friends had been. Emotional affairs, many had pointed out to him, were a lot more destructive than sex with someone outside the marriage. For that alone he was owed full custody.

Eve looked puzzled. "How would that have benefited Tiffany? She needs a mommy *and* a daddy, doesn't she?"

Glad to see she wasn't the vengeful type, Derek nodded gratefully.

"And you work full-time. And probably still travel," Eve continued.

"Although less than I did before," he said.

She compressed her lips, then took her last bite of crème brûlée and set the dish aside. "Having parents who rue each other's very existence is no help to anyone, believe me."

As interested in Eve as she apparently was in him,

Derek sat back in his chair and sipped his coffee. "And you know that because…?"

She got up and poured herself a cup of coffee, too. "My father wanted nothing to do with me, not when I was a kid or after I grew up."

Derek winced. "Wow. That's harsh."

Eve added cream, then sprinkled in a packet of sugar. She stirred the coffee, tasted it, then went back and sat down at the other end of the couch. "You get used to it. For a lot of years, I wished my mother and my biological father had gotten along. Then I began to accept that if they had no use for each other, it was really better that we never saw him. You, on the other hand, have managed to stay friends with your ex and her new husband. The fact you do get along can only benefit all seven of the kids involved."

Her ready understanding boosted Derek's morale. "So you don't think I was a fool?"

Eve shook her head. "I think you were noble." She flashed him an encouraging smile and continued to hold his gaze as she sipped her coffee. "No, I think you were realistic, that you did the right thing for everyone."

Not sure when he had enjoyed a woman's company this much, he smiled back at her. "Thanks."

"So." Her expression determined, Eve rose gracefully and headed to the desk where she'd set up her laptop computer. "Back to the house-hunting."

When Derek joined her, she glanced up at him from the computer. "I don't want to waste your time, but I really want you to look at more than one home." Before he could object, she continued firmly, "There are three immediately available properties in your stated price range in Highland Park, within a two-mile radius of Tiffany's other home. I've emailed you the specs on all three, to peruse at your leisure. Two are having unadvertised open houses tomorrow afternoon, for qualified buyers only. The other is available only by appointment. Would you like to hit all three at once tomorrow?"

Derek did—for reasons that didn't have as much to do with house-hunting as they should. "We'll have to take Tiffany with us," he warned.

Eve's expression softened in a way that let him know what a good mother she would be one day. "Shouldn't be a problem," she assured him confidently.

Derek watched her put her laptop back in the case. "Can we do it after her afternoon nap, say, at two-thirty?"

"Absolutely." Eve gathered up her belongings and headed for the door.

Derek walked with her. She hesitated in the entry, and for a brief moment he was tempted to kiss her. As if sensing it, Eve drew away. "I'll see you then," she said briskly, before moving off down the hall.

"YOU'RE LOOKING A lot better," Eve told her mother happily the next morning after arriving at the hospital to visit her.

Marjorie accepted with a smile the stack of magazines Eve had brought her. "How are things going with Derek McCabe?"

A little too well on the personal side, Eve thought uncomfortably. She moved a chair closer to the bed and sank into it. "We're looking at three properties this afternoon." Marjorie, who had every luxury listing in the area memorized, considered the plan thoughtfully as her daughter specified which ones they were seeing. "Is he going to be easy or difficult to please?"

In what way? Eve pushed the unexpectedly amorous

thought aside. "It's too soon to tell." All she knew for certain was that Derek had an enormous capacity for giving—to the point he probably had Christmas in his heart all year long. And Eve envied him that. She had trouble getting into the holiday spirit at all.

Marjorie paused. "I know I've said this before, but… be careful. I don't want to see you hurt."

Eve clasped her mom's hand, happy that she didn't seem as weak and fragile as she had the day before. "Believe me, I don't want to be hurt, either." One devastating love affair had been enough to last her a lifetime.

"You don't need a man in your life to be happy," her mother continued.

Oh, how well Eve knew that. She squeezed her mother's fingers. "You don't have to worry about it, Mom. Derek is just a client. I'm his real estate agent." She paused to let her words sink in. "And nothing more."

It didn't matter how physically and emotionally attracted she was to him, she thought. At the end of the transaction, she and Derek would go their separate ways. And that would be that.

Chapter Three

"Not exactly what you had in mind, hmm?" Eve asked Derek as they left house number two and headed down the long curving stone walk to his car. It was a beautiful December day with clear blue skies, and warm enough that only light jackets were required.

Derek turned to her. He had showered and shaved before meeting her, and he smelled of sandalwood and pine. "I've been in nice homes before, lots of them."

"But no open houses where free Botox injections were offered?"

He mimed a shudder and moved closer, the sunlight picking up the mahogany in his short dark hair. "I know plastic surgery and other enhancements are popular in Dallas," he said in a low voice. "But to do it as part of an open house…"

"A bit tacky?" she asked wryly.

"You got that right." He shifted Tiffany to his other arm while he fished for his keys.

Seeing he needed assistance, Eve held out her arms. She expected the tyke to slide into them as easily as she had the day before. Instead, Tiffany turned away and buried her face in her daddy's shoulder.

"Sorry," Derek murmured.

"No problem," Eve returned easily. She was about

to offer to help him reach his keys, but slipping her fingers into the jeans pocket adjacent to his fly did not seem like the best idea. She turned away to survey the beautifully landscaped lawn.

With Tiffany cuddled on his shoulder, Derek fished some more. He finally got what he needed and unlocked the doors. While he put Tiffany in her car seat, Eve slid into the passenger side of the Jaguar.

Yet another anomaly in this situation.

Normally, she drove clients around.

But since Tiffany's car seat was already in his SUV, and they were apparently a hassle to put in correctly, Derek preferred to do the driving.

He settled himself behind the wheel, grabbed his designer shades and adjusted them over his eyes. Which was a shame, Eve thought, because now she wouldn't be able to use his gaze to intuit what he was thinking; she'd have to rely on his body language and tone of voice to try to figure him out.

Stifling a sigh, she put on her own sunglasses to guard against the glare.

Derek stretched his right arm along the back of the front seats, turned to make sure all was clear and reversed out of the drive. "As if that Botox party wasn't weird enough…what was with the free massages at that first place?" He put the car in gear, then sat idling while Eve punched the address of their next possibility into the GPS built into the dashboard.

"It was part of the promotion for the property," Eve explained. "A way to get qualified buyers, ones who can afford a seven- or eight-million-dollar home, out to see it."

Derek drove off when the suggested route popped up on the screen. Shortly thereafter, he made the first turn. "The thinking being, if you actually tried out the home gym and the pool and the sport court, and then had a free massage…" He waited for a traffic jam on Mockingbird Lane to clear.

"And a catered lunch in the gourmet kitchen." Noticing her skirt had ridden up slightly on her thigh, Eve discreetly tugged it down. "You'd be hooked."

He shrugged. "It might work. If that was what you wanted." The home had a billiard room and a home theater, swimming pool and crowd-sized hot tub.

"I'm guessing it was too much of a bachelor pad for your taste." Even though it had been just down the street from his ex.

"It didn't exactly spell *family*," he agreed drily.

Eve brought out the specs she had previously sent him. She refreshed his memory with a few photos from the sales brochure while they sat at a stoplight. "You may like the next one."

"Daddy!"

Derek glanced at his daughter via the rearview mirror. She looked ready to start fussing at any moment. "Hi, honey," he said, turning around to smile at her briefly, before picking up the conversation where they'd left off. "I hope so," he stated quietly. "Tiffany's been a trouper, but she's really tired."

Unfortunately, the next property elicited as many frowns and scowls from both Derek and his little girl as the first two had. Luckily, there was no open house going on, so they were free to talk frankly. "What is it you don't like about it?" Eve asked, trying to get a handle on what it was Derek truly wanted in a home.

He walked around the huge rooms.

Part of the estate of a late oil tycoon, it had been built

in the early eighties, and recently staged and updated in sophisticated neutral palettes.

"Let me count the ways," he said, placating the little girl he held in his arms with the baby bottle of apple juice he'd brought in with them. "The marble floors are way too cold and hard. The floor plan is awful, and I think the spiral staircase could be dangerous for a kid."

Okay, Eve noted, that was a start.

She edged closer. "It's five streets over from your ex's home. The staircase could be replaced. And it has a nice big backyard with a fence, and room for a really nice play set."

Finished with her juice, Tiffany pushed the empty baby bottle at Eve, then reached out and touched Eve's hair. The little girl smiled as she got a fistful, and held on tight.

Afraid to move, Eve smiled back at her and stayed very still.

Derek came to the rescue, his touch tender as he extricated her from his daughter. Which in turn made Eve wonder what kind of lover he would be. Probably excellent, if her feminine intuition was any indication. Not that she should be thinking this way…

"It also has a pool," he continued, while Eve put the empty bottle back in the diaper bag slung over his broad shoulder. "I don't think I want a swimming pool with a toddler around, fenced or not. Maybe when she's older. Not now."

Aware that Tiffany was looking restless again, Eve rummaged in the diaper bag and found a set of plastic baby keys she could play with. "Pools can be taken out. The entire decor can be changed."

Tiffany grinned and shook the keys in both her tiny fists until they rattled.

Derek continued glancing around. "It would still be way too big."

As would all the properties in the seven- to eight-million-dollar range, Eve thought, since the asking price was directly related to the amount of square footage.

Trying to be helpful, she asked, "Do you want to look at something smaller?"

His jaw set in that stubborn way she was beginning to know so well. Tiffany grabbed the sunglasses tucked into the neckline of his cashmere sweater, shook them once and threw them to the floor. They landed with a clatter but, to Eve's relief, didn't break.

"I wanted there to be parity in our homes." Derek set Tiffany down on the floor. Happy to be able to flex her legs, she grabbed the keys and sunglasses and toddled happily around the foyer, babbling all the while.

"Okay," Eve said.

Derek blocked the way to the staircase, keeping an eye on his daughter while studying Eve shrewdly. "You don't agree with that objective, though."

There he went, putting her on the spot again. Although it wasn't always what a client wanted, Eve decided yet again to be honest. She shrugged and knelt down to engage Tiffany with another toy the little girl had previously discarded. "Your homes are going to be different, no matter the square footage and price tag."

Tiffany took the stuffed bunny and sat down on the floor to examine it.

Confident that the toddler was entertained, at least for the moment, Eve rose. She looked her handsome client in the eye and continued, "Carleen has a husband and seven kids, if you count Craig's. At your place, it's just going to be the two of you." Eve paused to let that fact sink in, and then forged on. "Tiffany is going to feel the difference. It doesn't mean she'll like one place any more or any less, especially at this age. Your home should reflect who you are, what *you* want, Derek. Not what Carleen and Craig need and want for their brood."

Tiffany stood and grabbed her daddy's jean-clad legs. "So something cozier." Derek smiled and picked her up.

His daughter nestled against his chest, as if in heaven, a reaction Eve could understand, given who Tiffany was nestling against. It had to feel great, being that close to Derek. She knew she would be happy with his big, strong arms wrapped around her.

"There are smaller homes in this area," she told him. "Some have been redone, some not. In any case, the price tag will be quite different." Which, Eve knew, could be a deal-breaker for a venture capitalist who also wanted a house as a monetary investment.

Derek squinted. "How different?"

"It depends on how small you want to go. Not to mention the overall condition of the property."

Derek sighed as Tiffany grabbed his sweater with both hands and let out an impatient shout. "Bye-bye!"

He headed out the door. "Meaning we have to keep looking."

Eve paused to lock up. "If you want to be happy with your choice, you do."

He glanced at his watch. "I have to take Tiffany back to Carleen."

It was almost five-thirty. "You want to call it a day, then?" Eve asked, unable to help but feel a little disappointed that their time together would soon be ending.

"Actually," he said, as if reading her mind and feeling the same way, "I'd like to keep looking tonight."

"Okay, then," Eve smiled. "Let's do it."

"I THINK WE should stop. At least for today," Eve said, an exhausting three hours later.

Darkness had fallen a long time ago. They had physically gone through two more homes, and driven by eight more, only to have Derek dismiss them out of hand for one reason or another.

"After a while, everything begins to blur together. We can start again tomorrow if you like." Plus, without Tiffany as a tiny chaperone and constant distraction, Eve found herself way too physically aware of her hunky client.

The only good thing was that once they had dropped his daughter off, they'd been able to swing by the office so she could pick up *her* car and do the driving. While Derek concentrated on perusing the neighborhoods from the passenger seat, she tried hard not to think about how intimate it felt to have him sitting so close beside her.

"What about that one?" His mind evidently where it should be, Derek pointed to a cozy English Tudor–style cottage with a for-sale sign in front.

Grateful for the latest diversion, Eve steered her car to the curb. Up and down the street, homes were lit up with Christmas lights. However, the one in front of them was dark and neglected. Familiar with the original 1960s interior, she warned, "It's a fixer-upper. Nowhere near move-in ready. And way below your target price."

Derek continued to stare at the ivy-covered brick. "I'd like to see it, anyway."

They wouldn't need an appointment; this property was on lockbox. She could let them in.

"Okay," Eve said, thinking that if anything were to end his desire to keep looking, this particular property would be it. She cut the ignition and led the way up to the front porch. Inside, it was worse than she remembered from the initial agents tour: chill and dank. Bad carpeting, outdated everything.

"What's the story on the property?" Derek asked.

She continued switching on overhead lights. "The owner has gone into a nursing home. The family isn't interested in doing anything to the house." Hence, it had been cleared of all belongings, but not staged or in any way adequately prepared for sale. "They're hoping it will go as a teardown."

He shot her a questioning look.

"Which means that someone will buy it for the lot—which is a premium—demolish this property and start from scratch," she explained.

Derek ran a hand over a wall in the study. He shook his head admiringly at the built-in bookshelves and ornate trim. "Look at this wood."

"Paneling's not really popular these days."

"I like it."

The client was always right. And it could be stripped and refinished to give it a more updated look. "It's very masculine."

He pivoted and regarded her speculatively, as if wondering if she was playing him.

She wasn't.

After a moment, he seemed to accept that.

Eve sobered. "I want you to see the kitchen, though."

They walked down the hall to the rear of the house. Eve hit another switch. Derek blinked at the orange-yellow-and-brown-plaid vinyl wallpaper. "Talk about a blast from the past," he murmured.

The laminate counters were also bright orange, the floor a speckled linoleum. "I know," Eve sympathized, looking past the grime-smeared windows and severely outdated appliances. "Really awful, hmm?"

He peered at a cobweb overhead. "It could use a good cleaning, that's for certain."

Eve moved her foot away from something sticky on the floor. "No joke."

Derek came closer. He stood next to her, thoughtfully looking around, his steady presence and the warmth of his tall, strong body a nice counterpoint to the lingering chill inside the home. "But with all new appliances…"

Ignoring the tingling deep inside her, along with the wish the two of them had met some other time, some other way, Eve drew a deep breath and pointed out the rest of the flaws. "It's going to need brand-new cabinets, counters, flooring and updated lighting, too." She turned abruptly, her shoulder bumping against his bicep. "The kitchen alone would cost you at least fifty thousand. Then there's the furnace and air conditioning, and it will also most likely need all new electrical and plumbing."

"How much are they asking?"

Doing her best to tamp down her continuing awareness, Eve showed him the listing information left on the kitchen counter. "One point five million, but that's too high for the condition of this house." She led the way up to the second floor. There were four nice-sized bedrooms and two full baths, one off the hall and one off the master bedroom.

Derek continued to look around with real interest. "What do you think it should be going for?"

Eve studied the worn carpeting and cramped, outdated bathrooms, the dingy walls and lack of adequate closet space. "One point two million, max. And that's mostly due to the location." She turned back to Derek, in full business mode, but found herself temporarily blinded by his brilliant blue eyes. "I'd, uh, be tempted to go in at one point one million, and then let them talk you back to one point two, as the most you would pay. Although, with your time frame, wanting to be in before Christmas, I can't recommend you take this on."

Derek stood, legs braced apart, hands on his waist, still looking around. "Surely you know contractors who would be willing to do whatever it took, particularly if bonus pay was involved."

He really was serious. "I do." Despite herself, Eve began to get excited, too.

Derek walked around some more, as if dreaming about what a good infusion of cash and a little tender loving care could do for this home. He swung back toward her. "Could you get it done in a week?"

Good heavens, the man was demanding! But all of a sudden willing to be ambitious, too, Eve straightened her spine and replied, "Maybe two, if we come to terms with the sellers right away, and you're willing to pay time and a half for the entire job."

He shrugged off the problem. "I'm okay with that."

They finished looking around the bedrooms and went back downstairs. "Why this house?" she asked curiously, turning off another bank of lights.

Derek shook his head. He prowled the first floor, his expression thoughtful. "I don't know. Something about the way it looks. Feels." He turned to her with a grin, certain now. "I want to put an offer in tonight."

Eve studied him. She hated snap decisions when it came to something this important. "You're sure this is what you want?" she asked finally.

Derek nodded.

The light in his eyes, his sheer enthusiasm, were irresistible. *Okay, then.* They went back to her office again.

Eve called the other Realtor to let her know an offer was coming in, and then wrote up the contract. She had barely faxed it over when her cell phone rang. Derek's offer, to take the house as is, without inspection, had been accepted.

He grinned. "Looks like I just bought myself a house!" he said, wrapping Eve in a warm, Texas-style hug. It was the kind of embrace people gave each other after the winning goal in a football game. Yet the brief expression of exaltation left her tingling and on edge long after they broke apart.

Eve congratulated Derek again, more formally this time, and then bid him good-night. It was a good thing her business with Derek McCabe was almost over. She was going to have a hard enough time forgetting the powerful attraction she felt for him as it was.

EVE WAS STILL thinking about the congratulatory hug from Derek—and her unprecedented reaction to it—when she went to the hospital the next morning to help with her mother's transfer.

As expected, even though the facility was bright and cheerful, Marjorie was less than enthusiastic about her upcoming stay in the cardiac rehab unit.

"I'd rather just go home," she grumbled, accepting the bag of comfortable clothing Eve had brought her.

Aware of the irony in taking on the parental role in their relationship, Eve handed over her mother's computer tablet and the weekend newspapers. "This is a necessary part of your recovery, Mom." Although she doubted her mother would change anything about her life without putting up a heck of a fight.

Marjorie made a face and removed the real estate inserts from both papers. "Have you found Derek Mc-Cabe a house yet?"

Grateful for the change of subject, Eve gave her the details.

Her mom blinked. "I thought he was in the market for an eight-million-dollar home!"

Eve knew a transaction of that magnitude would have likely given them a solid lead in the annual sales race. Refusing to feel guilty for doing what was right for her client, however, she explained, "He decided he wanted something much smaller in scope and more baby-friendly. The good news is he's very happy."

Or at least he had been the night before. Eve still had the feeling it was all happening a little too fast for comfort.

Her sense of foreboding increased the next day.

She had been given permission to get contractors in to look at the property in advance of the closing, and she went to the house to let them in. By the time they'd finished, Derek had arrived. The kitchen and bath designer, plumber, electrician, flooring rep and painters all conferred with him, and promised to have formal estimates for him the following morning.

Bad news relayed, they filed out, one by one.

Leaving Derek and Eve alone.

"So what do you think?" she asked, looking around at the empty house. The heating and ventilation system was out of commission, so the interior was chilly and dank. A light rain was falling, and on this gloomy December day the house seemed even more in need of tender loving care. "Feel overwhelmed yet?"

Derek shook his head. "Excited."

Glad to see he hadn't changed his mind about his

spur-of-the-moment decision, because deep down she sensed that this was indeed the perfect home for him, she allowed herself to tease, "And here you thought you weren't the fixer-upper type."

He gave her a leisurely once-over. "Sometimes it's necessary to get business out of the way. So you can move on to more important things."

Puzzled, Eve tilted her head. "Like what?"

The look he gave her was direct, uncompromising, confident. "Asking you out."

For a second, she was certain she hadn't heard right. The sparkle in his eyes told her that she had. Her pulse pounding, Eve worked to get air into her lungs. "On a date?" she asked hoarsely.

His sexy smile widening, he inched closer. "That was the general idea," he said.

Eve pressed her palm to her chest, trying to tamp down the immediate spark of excitement she felt. "I'm flattered."

Derek sobered. "I don't want you to be flattered," he told her huskily. He took her in his arms and pulled her flush against him. "I want you to say yes."

Chapter Four

Yes was what Eve wanted, too. Even if she would have preferred not to admit it. Before she could stop herself, before she could think of all the reasons why not, she let Derek pull her closer still. His head dipped. Her breath caught, and her eyes closed. And then all was lost in the first luscious feeling of his lips lightly pressed against hers.

It was a cautious kiss. A gentle kiss that didn't stay gallant for long. At her first quiver of sensation, he flattened his hands over her spine and deepened the kiss, seducing her with the heat of his mouth and the sheer masculinity of his tall, strong body. Yearning swept through her in great enervating waves. Unable to help herself, Eve went up on tiptoe, leaning into his embrace. Throwing caution to the wind, she wreathed her arms about his neck and kissed him back. Not tentatively, not sweetly, but with all the hunger and need she felt. And to her wonder and delight, he kissed her back in kind, again and again and again.

Derek had only meant to show Eve they had chemistry. Amazing chemistry that would convince her to go out with him, at least once. He hadn't expected to feel tenderness well inside him, even as his body went hard with desire. He hadn't expected to want to make love to her here and now, in this empty house. But sensing that total surrender would be a mistake, he tamped down his own desire and let the kiss come to a slow, gradual end.

Eve stepped backward, too, a mixture of surprise and pleasure on her face. Her breasts were rising and falling quickly, and her lips were moist. Amazement at the potency of their attraction, and something else a lot more cautious, appeared in her eyes. Eve drew a breath, and then anger flashed. "That was a mistake."

Derek understood her need to play down what had just happened, even as he saw no reason to pretend they hadn't enjoyed themselves immensely. "Not in my book," he murmured, still feeling a little off balance himself. In fact, he was ready for a whole lot more.

She held up a finger and shook it. Composed again, she stalked away from him, her high heels echoing on the wood floor. When she swung around to face him, he could tell her every defense was in place. "What you're feeling right now is all related to the roller-coaster emotions of buying a new home. One minute you're up, the next you're down. The euphoria you just felt is going to be very short-lived."

Like hell it was! He was adult enough to know the difference between being excited about purchasing a home, and wanting to make a woman his. And so was she. He rocked back on his heels, braced his hands on his waist and sent her an impudent grin. "You're telling me you've been kissed by clients at the end of a deal before?"

"Yes," Eve said. She looked him in the eye, long and hard. "I have."

HER MATTER-OF-FACT confession had served its purpose. First, Derek looked shell-shocked, then skeptical, and finally, as she had hoped, blatantly unhappy. He stepped closer, as if that would change anything. "You're kidding," he exclaimed in a low, raspy voice that practically oozed testosterone.

Eve struggled not to get swept up in the moment or the man, as embarrassment warmed her cheeks. "I wish."

He shifted forward, invading her space. "How many times?"

With effort, she kept her gaze locked with his. Determined to handle a situation that was fast escalating out of control, she replied, "Including you?"

He nodded.

"Twice."

Derek looked at her as if he already knew what it would be like to make love to her. "There must be more to the story," he said.

Since the last thing she needed to be doing was thinking about kissing him again, or worse, imagining what it would be like to make love with him, Eve lifted her chin and drew a deep, calming breath. Refusing to fixate on the fact that everywhere he was hard, she would be soft, or that everywhere he was male, she'd be female, she challenged, "Really. What makes you think that?"

Regarding her with a devil-may-care glint in his eyes, he pointed out, "You're not the kind of woman who lets her guard down easily."

That was certainly true. Although she wished he had not intuited the fact.

"So what happened, the other time?" Derek continued, a tad impatiently.

Eve shrugged and kept her voice matter-of-fact. "I was fresh out of real estate school. Ryan was a classmate of mine, from Southern Methodist University. He had just come into his trust fund and wanted to buy a bachelor pad in Deep Elum. It wasn't my area of expertise, but the commission was going to be great if I could find what he wanted. Ryan, of course, had no idea what that was, so we had to do quite a lot of looking together." Eve paused, recalling how naive and hopelessly romantic she had been at the time.

Working to keep the disillusionment out of her tone, she admitted, "One thing led to another, and by the time Ryan closed on his new loft, it was clear there was something between us. Or so we thought."

The chivalrous, protective look was back in Derek's eyes. "What happened?" he prodded.

"Exactly what you would think," Eve stated, with a cavalier attitude she couldn't begin to really feel. *My heart was broken and my spirits were crushed.* "Ryan and I came to the mutual conclusion that it had all happened too fast. We didn't have nearly as much in common as we'd thought, so we ended it. And," Eve continued, without the slightest bit of irony, "I learned a valuable lesson."

Derek regarded her gently. "Which was?"

She appreciated his understanding, even as she forced herself to take another step away from him. "I'll never again make the mistake of thinking the intimacy that develops during a home search will continue once a residence is found." She splayed a hand across her chest again. "I'm a Realtor. You're my client." She paused to let her words sink in. "And that is all."

She tensed as the first notes of the country ballad "Need You Now" emanated from her cell phone: Loughlin Realty's emergency ring. "Excuse me." Eve plucked her phone out of her bag and stalked off. "I've got to get this."

Sasha, the office manager, was on the other end.

Eve listened, hardly able to believe what was being said about her mother. "She *what?*" Her heart sank. "No! My God, no!" Then she commanded quickly, "Don't do that. Tell her I'll be right there! Yes, I'm five minutes away, max. Just hold her off, Sasha. Please."

Almost as distraught as she'd been the day of her mother's heart attack, Eve ended the call and grabbed her carryall.

"Everything okay?" Derek followed her, obviously concerned.

Aware she'd already been way too intimate with him, she kept him at arm's length. "I've got an emergency back at the office," she told him calmly. "You can stay as long as you like. Just lock up before you go, and return the key to the office."

"You're sure everything is okay?"

It wasn't, but what could she say besides the obvious? "I'm sorry, Derek, I've got to go."

Giving him no further chance to question her, Eve rushed out the door.

THE HOUSE WAS oddly silent and gloomy after Eve's abrupt departure. Not certain what had happened, but accepting her implication that it was none of his business, Derek walked around, switching off lights and making sure all the doors were locked. He had almost finished the task when he saw Eve's red-leather-bound iPad sitting on the counter next to the various contractor estimates. She'd left it behind in her haste to get out the door.

He glanced at his watch and saw it was five-thirty.

More than likely someone would still be at the office. And he had to return the key in any case.

He finished locking up, got in his car and drove over there. There were two cars in the lot, one of them Eve's white Mercedes sedan. A taxi was just pulling away. Inside the building, Sasha, the office manager, was in the reception area. The mid-thirtyish woman was as eclectically dressed as always, in a vivid handkerchief hem dress and lace-up high-heeled boots. Face pale, tight platinum curls standing on end, she was pacing and wringing her hands.

In Marjorie Loughlin's private office, voices rose.

"Mom, you can't do this!" Eve was insisting emotionally. "You *know* what the doctor said."

The well-coiffed woman beside her retorted, "I have a client I've been wooing for months coming in later this week."

"I know that, Mom," Eve replied in a soul-weary voice Derek had never heard her use before.

Eve's mother bulldozed on, pacing the office in much the same way Derek had seen Eve do. "And someone has to talk some sense into Flash Lefleur and get his condo adequately staged. Otherwise, who knows if and when his place will ever sell? And with only two weeks left on the listing contract!" Marjorie threw up her bejeweled hands. "I really don't want to let that one go, Eve."

"I told you I would take care of that, too," her daughter said plaintively.

"I want to believe you, honey. But...with all we have at stake here. Especially after what happened with the other sale..." The older woman's voice trailed off when she saw Derek standing in the doorway.

It was hard to figure out who looked worse, Derek

thought. Marjorie Loughlin was pale to the point of being gray, and a little physically shaky to boot. Eve looked anxious and distressed.

"May I help you?" the older woman asked, suddenly all genteel Southern charm.

Eve jumped in to make introductions. "Mom, this is Derek McCabe. Derek, my mother, Marjorie Loughlin. I don't think the two of you met when you came in the other day."

They hadn't, Derek realized.

Marjorie came forward to shake his hand. "Mr. McCabe, what a pleasure to meet you! Eve tells me you went to contract on a house."

Not really surprised by the zero-to-sixty change in attitude and demeanor—salespeople were legendary for their ability to morph into what was required—he nodded and returned her energetic smile. "I did. Your daughter was amazing, by the way."

"That's always good to hear," Marjorie replied, a bead of perspiration appearing on her elegant brow.

After a tense look at her mother, Eve stepped forward in turn. "What can we help you with?" she asked in a pleasant but businesslike tone.

He lifted the iPad in its red leather case, glad his presence had stopped the familial quarreling, at least momentarily. "You left this at the house."

Eve slanted a glance at her mother, who seemed to be swaying slightly. "Thank you for bringing it."

Before her daughter could get to her, Marjorie eased into the chair behind her impressive glass-and-chrome desk.

Noticing the way she was trembling, Eve turned paler, too. And it was easy to see why she was worried, Derek thought. Marjorie seemed near physical collapse, though she was trying her best to hide it. "Mrs. Loughlin, are you feeling all right?" he asked with concern.

"I don't see how Marjorie could be, since she just got out of the hospital," Sasha cried, obviously near tears.

"And she's supposed to be in the cardiac rehabilitation unit as we speak," Eve added pointedly.

Although she was ghostly white, and shaking visibly, Marjorie glared at her daughter and the stressed-out office manager. "I don't need it."

Eve glowered back, seeming to forget for a moment they had an audience. "That's not what I heard, Mom. I just spoke to your cardiologist, and Dr. Jackson said you checked yourself out against medical advice!"

Another dot of perspiration appeared on Marjorie's forehead, but she wiped it away. "I told the cardiac rehab staff I'd go when my schedule clears up. Right now—" she squared her shoulders and turned to the stack of messages on her desk "—there is work to be done here."

Eve paced, looking ready to explode. "Work the four other employees of the agency can handle."

Once again, Derek stepped in as peacemaker. "How long were you supposed to be at the rehab center?" he asked.

Marjorie shrugged and didn't answer.

"Four weeks," Eve said. "Then she's to continue her physical therapy on an outpatient basis and recuperate at home, until Dr. Jackson gives her the all-clear to return to work, which will probably be not until well after the Christmas holidays."

Derek had been through something similar with his own mother, when pneumonia precluded Josie's return to work. He poured Marjorie a glass of sparkling water and took it to her. Knowing it was sometimes easier to listen to a neutral third party than a family member, he said gently, "That's not too much to ask, is it? To follow medical advice, if for no other reason than to prevent any more issues with your heart?"

The older woman hesitated, but still did not give in.

Eve came and knelt down beside Marjorie, clasping her hands. "Come on, Mom. It *is* the season of giving, after all. And the only gift I want from you…is for you to be well." Still gazing up at her mother, she released a deep, quivering breath. And then burst into tears.

"THANK YOU SO much for all you did this evening," Eve told Derek two hours later, when they finally got back to the office. She glanced across the car at him as he pulled into the parking lot, then paused, her shoulder bag on her lap. "If you hadn't been here, using all your McCabe charm, I don't know if I would have been able to get my mother back to the cardiac rehabilitation center at all."

With the motor still idling, Derek reached across the leather console and took her hand in his. "The important thing is she went, and agreed to stay the duration, providing you take care of everything else. But my question is…" Derek paused, his warm palm still engulfing hers "…who's taking care of *you?*"

Eve caught her breath. Once again, her time with him was not going according to script. "What do you mean?"

"Did you even eat dinner last night?"

Eve didn't know how he could look so cool, calm and collected, when she felt so frazzled. "I…" She paused in turn, unable to remember when she'd eaten last. Warming to his slow, sexy smile, she had to admit reluctantly, "Maybe not."

As if they had all the time in the world to spend together, he continued his tender inquiry. "Breakfast this morning?"

Aware it had been forever since someone had taken care of her, she flushed, and pushed aside the memory of his kiss. "Toast."

He gave her a long, steady look. "Lunch?"

Eve fought back a second wave of heat. "A salad."

"Then you definitely need a solid meal this evening."

Trying not to think about how good it would feel to have a man like Derek looking after her, Eve folded her arms and retorted, "Since when did you become my personal nutritionist?"

He lifted his wide shoulders and she caught a whiff of his sandalwood-and-pine cologne. "Think of it as me returning all the favors you've done me the past few days."

Eve swallowed around the sudden tightness of her throat. "That was my job."

Triumph radiated in his smile. "And at the moment, being a gentleman is mine. Come on." He leaned toward her. "You know a good meal will not just fuel your body, but enable you to care for your mother and work a whole lot more efficiently to boot."

Unable to dispute all that he was saying, Eve lifted her hands in surrender. "Okay, I'll go." She held his gaze resolutely. "So long as we're both clear this is absolutely not a date."

Derek appeared affronted. "Of course not." His eyes twinkled. "It's just me saying thank-you to my most excellent Realtor."

Considering the size of the commission she was going to reap from the sale, Eve was the one expressing gratitude. "No. *I* am taking *you* out, as a thank-you."

His lips quirking with amusement, Derek put the Jaguar in reverse. "We'll fight over the check at dinner."

"No, we won't," Eve said calmly. "Because I'm buying."

It was, she knew, the best way to set an all-business tone for the evening. And prevent another kiss, or any emotional closeness from materializing again.

UNFORTUNATELY, THE RESTAURANT Derek chose felt anything but businesslike. It was dark and romantic, with deep leather booths that afforded maximum privacy. Adding to the winter wonderland atmosphere were abundant Christmas decorations and soothing holiday music playing in the background. Not to mention the sense that, despite her insistence to the contrary, this was in fact their first real date.

"So I take it you have no siblings," Derek said once the butternut bisque had been served.

Telling herself there could be no harm in getting acquainted in a friendly way—doing so might even eventually lead to more clients, upon his recommendation—Eve drew her spoon through the Granny Smith apple garnish. "No, it's always been just me and my mom."

He regarded her with interest. "Your mom never married?"

Trying not to feel a thrill at being with him in such an intimate setting, Eve shook her head and continued holding his gaze. "She never really even dated. The situation with my father turned her away from that. Although she insists it was really the best thing for her."

Derek poured them both a little more wine, an inscrutable expression on his face. "Do you agree with that assumption?"

Eve shrugged, not sure. "The please-go-away-and-never-darken-my-doorstep-again check my blue-blooded father gave her enabled her to get a foothold here and launch what has been a very satisfying career for her."

From the look of admiration he sent her way, Derek seemed to understand what a feat that had been for Marjorie, who'd come from nothing herself. "Does she want the same kind of life for you?"

"You mean single, high-powered career woman?" *Workaholic?* Eve added silently.

He nodded.

Good question. She finished her soup and moved the dish aside, giving his inquiry the serious consideration it deserved. "Well, she wants me to be able to support myself. She'd like it if I took over the business when she's gone."

Derek's gaze roved Eve's face, hair and lips, before returning ever so slowly to her eyes. "You don't see your mom stepping down?"

Tingling everywhere his gaze had landed, as well as everywhere it hadn't, Eve shook her head facetiously. "Not as long as there's breath in her body."

He chuckled. "Having met your mom, I totally understand. Mine is the same way."

They leaned back as their soup dishes were cleared and plates of vinaigrette-dressed field greens peppered with pecans and cranberries were set in front of them.

Derek regarded Eve curiously. "What about you? Do you want to have more of a personal life?" He waggled his brows comically. "Are you dating anyone?"

His exaggerated interest had her rolling her eyes. "Checking to see if there's any competition?"

"Something like that," he said smoothly.

Trying not to think about the way he looked at her—as if she was the most fascinating woman on the planet—Eve sipped her wine. "There is no one in the picture."

"No one you find interesting?" he pressed.

Except you? "Not even marginally."

He smiled in satisfaction, clearly not about to give up on his pursuit of her.

Ignoring her inner burst of excitement, and figuring it was her turn to ask questions, Eve said casually, "What about you? Have you dated since your divorce?"

"Some."

She didn't know why she found that disappointing. Keeping her gaze matter-of-fact, she prodded, "And?"

His lips compressed. "I have to say, up to now my heart really hasn't been in it."

Up to now. "You've been going through the motions." Eve understood. She'd done her fair share of that, too.

"But I've been going along with it, for my family's sake," Derek continued.

Now they were getting somewhere. "They want to see you married again."

He grimaced. "Very much so. To the point they'd like to see me sign up for services with my sister-in-law, Alexis. She's a professional matchmaker for Foreverlove.com."

Another alarm bell sounded in Eve's head. She welcomed the arrival of their entrees, which served as a distraction. "You're resisting, I take it?" she asked when the waiter was gone again.

Derek nodded and cut into his steak. "I prefer a less orchestrated approach."

Her gaze swept over his handsome face. "Meaning...?"

"On paper, my marriage to Carleen should have worked."

Eve had to fight the urge to reach over and take his hand. "But it didn't."

His eyes drifted to the pulse throbbing in her throat. "Maybe the key is finding someone not so much like yourself. Maybe that's the way to a happy ending."

Eve wasn't so sure about that. The only thing she did know for certain was that she and Derek were very different. In their backgrounds, in their wants and needs and most definitely in their outlooks on life.

"YOU'RE LOOKING BETTER this morning," Marjorie murmured when Eve went to the cardiac rehab to have breakfast with her.

Eve felt better after her leisurely dinner with Derek the night before.

She'd slept well, too, and to her consternation, awoke dreaming of kissing him again.

Not that Derek had made a move on her the night before. He'd been a perfect gentleman when he had taken her back to her car after dinner. Which was, after all, what she had wanted.

Wasn't it?

"I'm glad," Marjorie continued. "I was worried about you last night."

"Same here," Eve murmured, looking her over with the same close regard.

Clearly, there were improvements here, too.

Marjorie was dressed in workout clothes for the physical therapy she'd be doing later. Although she wore no makeup, her color was actually a lot better this morning than it had been at the office the previous afternoon. "I gather you had a good night's sleep?"

"Probably because Loughlin Realty is still in the lead in sales. Although—" Marjorie frowned "—maybe not for long. Sibley & Smith is set to go to contract on two more properties this morning, which, unfortunately, would put them only one point seven million dollars behind us." *In other words,* Eve thought, *one luxury property.*

"How do you know this?" she demanded, narrowing her eyes suspiciously.

Marjorie pushed the cottage cheese and fruit around on her plate. "I still have my ear to the ground."

Everything fell into place when Eve spotted the BlackBerry that was peeking out of her mom's pocket. Her appetite suddenly almost nonexistent, too, Eve nibbled on a whole wheat pancake provided by the cafeteria. "You're supposed to avoid stress, Mom."

Marjorie scoffed. "Keeping an eye on my business is a lot easier on me than being kept in the dark."

Unfortunately, Eve knew that was true. "I'll make the sale to Red Bloom happen, Mom." The Houston oilman not only loved collecting unique homes, he had tons of money to spend.

An imperious brow arched. "That's what you promised when it came to Derek McCabe."

"And I did find a property for him. One he's very excited about." Although Eve still felt Derek had rushed into the deal, and might end up regretting it if everything didn't go the way he hoped.

Marjorie sneaked a peek at her BlackBerry. "I would have preferred he be excited about an eight-million-dollar listing."

Eve stifled a groan. She liked to put property under contract as much as the next agent, but didn't want the sales race to dominate her life. "Mom. Please. It's

Christmastime. Let's stop worrying about competition. And work on finding the joy in our lives."

Marjorie slid her phone back into her pocket. She peered closely at Eve. "Since when did you become so romantic?"

Eve flushed.

"Or maybe," Marjorie continued, even more sagely, "I should ask who is responsible for making you see the world this way?"

There was only one answer to that, Eve knew. And she sensed her mother knew it, too.

Derek McCabe.

Chapter Five

Derek's rancorous business meeting the following day was in direct contrast to his incredibly enjoyable dinner with Eve. The young entrepreneurs sat on the other side of Derek's desk, looking crestfallen when he finished his in-depth analysis of their pitch. "So in other words, you're not going to fund us," the lead programmer said with obvious resentment.

This was the part of the job Derek loathed. He regarded the trio of budding geniuses. "As I said, your ideas are great. The business plan is not."

"How do we fix that?" the more amenable software designer asked.

"Find an executive with experience running a small software company, and a chief financial officer, to help set things up."

The marketing guru shook her head vehemently. "We don't need someone already set in his or her ways telling us what to do! The whole point of starting our own company is so we can run things ourselves!"

Knowing he'd done what he could to set them on the right path, Derek stood and shook their hands in turn. "Then I wish you luck," he said.

But they wouldn't be getting any venture capital from his company.

Alma May, his fifty-something administrative assistant, popped her head in the door after the surly trio departed. "Your parents called while you were in the meeting. They said they'd catch up with you later."

Aware his folks would probably be full of questions about the house he was buying when they did end up talking, Derek nodded.

His family would also be full of questions about Eve, if they had any inkling how interested he was in the pretty real estate agent. Luckily, they hadn't a clue. Derek wanted to keep it that way. Pursuing her was going to be a delicate business. She was cautious to a fault, overburdened with work and worried sick about her mom.

Hence, it wasn't an ideal time to jump-start a romance, Derek rationalized. And yet, to wait would risk losing what momentum they had gained.

Oblivious to the direction of his thoughts, Alma tossed her springy silver curls as she continued going down her list. "I rescheduled your appointments, as requested, so your afternoon is free."

Derek wondered if Eve would have any spare time, too. He wouldn't mind taking her out to lunch. Since she'd paid for dinner the night before, this would be his treat. And since the transaction would be closed by then, there would be nothing stopping them from interacting in a purely social way. Except, of course, Eve's theory about it being only the house-hunting that had brought them together.

"The bank called. They have the cashier's check ready for the closing. Which is…" his assistant consulted her watch "…in forty-five minutes."

Derek shut down his computer, glad to be done in the office for the day. He smiled. "I'm headed there now."

Eve was waiting for him, gorgeous as ever. She was wearing an elegant business suit with a black watch plaid skirt, dark green silk blouse and fitted black blazer. Black tights and matching suede heels set off her sexy, spectacular legs.

One thing that was different about her today, Derek noted appreciatively, was her hair. The silky golden-brown strands had been brushed off her face and twisted into a chignon at the nape of her neck. On another woman, the sophisticated style would have highlighted imperfections. However, on Eve, it pointed out the lack of them. From the oval shape of her face, to her wide-set amber eyes, straight nose, chiseled cheekbones and full, bow-shaped lips, she was absolute perfection.

Derek knew it. And it was evident that the sellers, the attorneys and even the other Realtor involved knew it as well. Only Eve seemed oblivious to just how lovely she was.

Derek promised to remedy that as soon as humanly possible. But first things first; they had to close on the property.

Two hours later, it was a done deal. The lawyers and sellers departed. Hal Brody, the listing agent for the other party, stayed behind to tie up loose ends. After taking the lockbox off the door, he glanced over at Eve. "Congratulations. Looks like Loughlin Realty is going to win. Talk is, despite their recent sales, Sibley & Smith is still going to fall short."

With a pleasant smile fixed on her face, Eve cautioned her colleague, "Let's not be too hasty, Hal. As you and I both know, anything can happen, especially this time of year."

He went to get the real estate stand out of the front yard. "Well, just so you know, since it can't be us," the distinguished-looking Realtor said as he returned, "I'm rooting for your team."

"Thanks, Hal," Eve replied. But her expression indicated they would just have to see what developed.

"Pleasure doing business with you, as always." Hal slid the sold sign into his trunk.

Behind them, a familiar canary-yellow truck pulled up to the curb. Derek's heart sank. As much as he loved the occupants, he did not need this now.

Eve caught his expression and frowned. "Expecting company?" she asked quietly as Hal waved and took off.

"No," Derek said, but after his email announcing his plans the day before, he should have guessed his parents would show up in person, rather than just call him at the office.

Smiling and waving, his parents got out of the pickup. As always, they made a handsome couple. The kind you could look at and just know they belonged together, and always had. It was that kind of comfort and compatibility that Derek wanted, too.

Beside him, he felt Eve's attention turn to his folks. She seemed curious—obviously, she hadn't put two and two together yet, and wondered what he had in common with this couple—yet she appeared as welcoming as always.

Derek understood. He was standing here in a suit and tie, having just come from his downtown Dallas office. His mom was dressed in her usual jeans, boots and wool jacket. His dad, also in jeans and boots, had a shearling-lined suede jacket on, a black Stetson slanted across his brow. Both looked very West Texas and proud of it.

"Eve, I'd like you to meet my parents, Josie and Wade McCabe. Mom, Dad, this is Eve Loughlin, the Realtor who negotiated the purchase of my new home."

Josie greeted Eve warmly, and then turned back to Derek. Wade did the same. "I gather the closing went without a hitch, then?" she asked.

Derek tried not to notice the hint of disappointment in his mother's eyes. "Usually does when you pay cash for a property," he quipped.

Another glint of disappointment appeared.

Ever the peacemaker between Derek and his mom, his dad stepped in like clockwork. Wade's years successfully investing in troubled companies of all kinds had given him an ability to talk affably with everyone, no matter what the circumstances. "Want to show us around?" he asked Eve.

Derek knew the agenda here. His mother wanted to talk to him alone, as she always handled the "emotional" issues in the family. His dad would get to know Eve, and figure out what, if anything, she had to do with his hasty actions.

Apparently unwilling to get swept up into his family drama, however, Eve lifted a hand and took a step backward. "Actually, I should be going—"

"Actually," Derek cut in, "if you have a minute, Eve, I'd really like you to stay." He knew his parents were worried about him. They'd been concerned ever since he had given up on his marriage without a fight. He just didn't want to hear about it.

Derek pivoted to Eve, awaiting her decision.

Their eyes met and held. "Certainly," she said at last, with a look that conceded she owed him when it came to running interference with family. "I'd be glad to help out in whatever way I can."

EVE WASN'T SURE what was going on between Derek and his folks. She did know they were the last people he had wanted to see at that particular moment. And if his tense body language was any indication, that feeling seemed to intensify when his parents stepped into his new home and had their first look around.

Clearly, they were in shock as they scoped it out. Wondering, even if they were too polite to actually come out and say so, what in the world Derek had done.

Finally, Josie drew a deep breath. "It will be a wonderful home when it's redone."

Wade nodded as he strolled through the downstairs. He looked out at the spacious backyard through a bank of grimy single-pane windows that were definitely going to have to be replaced. "I think so, too."

"But what are you going to do in the meantime?" his mother asked. "I thought you wanted to be out of the hotel by the holidays." Her youthful face radiated concern. "For Tiffany's sake."

"And I will be," Derek promised.

Josie's gaze narrowed in a way that let Eve know this woman would not accept any useless excuses from her son. "Surely you know that you can't have a baby around ongoing renovation."

"It's going to be finished by Christmas, Mom, with a week to spare." Derek went on to state in excruciating detail what all was going to be done.

Josie and Wade stared at him as if he had lost his mind. "That will all be finished two weeks from now?" his mother repeated with a mixture of shock and disbelief.

Derek nodded. "They've promised."

More alarmed looks transferred between his folks.

"I know what tradespeople say," Josie declared. "But when it comes to renovations there are *always* unexpected delays. You cannot go by the best-case-scenario estimates, son."

Derek folded his arms across his chest. "Eve has assured me that won't be an issue with these particular contractors."

Josie turned back to her, and Eve had an idea what it would be like to be at the top of Josie's Not Happy With list. Sighing inwardly, she couldn't help but sympathize with Derek. It was the same with her mother. As long as they felt you were on the right path, all was golden. The minute you weren't...Mama Bear personality returned.

Once again, Derek's dad stepped in to calmly defuse the situation. "How about you show me the upstairs?" he suggested. The upshot being so Derek and his mom could talk.

Knowing he was no more likely to get out of that than she was to avoid her own mother's scrutiny, Eve smiled despite herself.

Feeling as if she had unwittingly stumbled into a hornet's nest, she said, "I'd be glad to."

The rumbling of voices continued while she and Wade looked around the second floor. Eve took her time explaining what Derek had planned for each room.

"Naturally, he also has an interior designer helping him pick out the soothing, neutral color scheme he wants. She will get it move-in ready for Derek and Tiffany, right down to the dishes and the towels. All Derek will have to do is turn the key and walk in."

"That's good. Interior design isn't exactly the forte of any of our sons."

Eve hesitated, reluctant to insert herself into a situation where she didn't belong, yet wanting to assist Derek in alleviating his parents' worry. "I know how disconcerting it looks now, but knowing what kind of relaxed and easy home life he wants, I think Derek's made a very good choice, as well as a sound financial investment."

"With the exception that it is well under my son's initial financial goal."

"I don't think it's an issue as far as his portfolio goes, since Derek still plans to invest more money in real estate by the end of the year. Besides, it's close to Carleen, close to Derek's work." Even close to Eve's office and her condo. Not that she should be thinking that way...

Wade smiled. "I think Derek's chosen wisely, too," he said quietly, in that instant looking very much like his son. "Maybe more than he knows or realizes."

Eve wasn't sure what Derek's father meant by that.

Wade frowned, continuing, "I think the real issue is that he had told us a while back that his next home was going to be a ranch, so that Tiffany would be able to enjoy the outdoors as much as he did when he was a kid."

Caught off guard, yet trying her best to hide it, Eve shrugged. "He didn't say anything about that to me...."

"That's what worries us," Wade returned. "Not that it matters what the plan was. Apparently, there's a different one now." Lips compressed, the older man turned and headed for the stairs.

The air was thick with tension when they rejoined the others in the living room.

"You're sure you won't have lunch with us?" Josie asked Derek, clearly trying to make amends.

He shook his head, his shoulders as set as the expression on his face. "I already have plans. Maybe another time, Mom."

Josie searched his face. "We will see you for the family Christmas party, though."

Derek nodded. His current aggravation with them notwithstanding, he clearly loved and respected both his parents. "I made arrangements with Carleen to take Tiffany to Laramie for the weekend before Christmas," he reassured them.

Josie smiled. "Good." Her expression gentled. "My favorite time of year is when I have all you boys with us." She gave her big, strapping son a fiercely maternal hug, then stepped back and gave him another long, beseeching look. "Don't be too angry with me."

Derek exhaled, his irritation back full force. "Got to let us go, Mom," was all he said in return. He shook his head in silent remonstration. *"You've got to let us go."*

EVE WAITED UNTIL the elder McCabes had departed, then turned back to Derek. From her shoulder bag she withdrew an envelope with his name scrawled across the front.

"Well, thank you again for choosing Loughlin Realty," she said formally.

Derek accepted the envelope she pushed into his hands. He opened it, saw the thank-you and the gift card for a five-star restaurant, and smiled in satisfaction. "This means our business is done?"

Suddenly wishing her reasons for being around Derek weren't over, Eve forced herself to stay professional. "As far as the closing goes. Naturally, if you encounter any post-sale problems, I'd like to know. We want you to be happy with the final result." How many times had she said these same words? And felt relieved, not sad?

Derek paused, as if choosing his words carefully. Finally, he said, "I am happy."

Their gazes met. Eve could see that was true—about the sale. As for other aspects of his life, he was not as pleased. She walked back upstairs with him, checking the rooms, making sure the lights were turned off, the shades pulled.

Wanting him to put his thoughts and feelings into words, she continued, "I'm sorry your parents weren't thrilled with your choice of a home."

In no hurry to leave, he sat down on a seat built into the wide shed window in the master bedroom. "You weren't either, so long ago."

Eve moved closer, so they wouldn't have to talk as loud, and leaned against the wall.

Outside, the sun was peeking through the winter gloom, sending splintered rays into the master suite. The light caught the dark strands of Derek's short, rumpled hair, bringing out glints of brown and maple. She could see how closely he had shaved that morning, as well as how deep blue his eyes were, how masculine his features. She could never tire of looking at him, being with him. Which was, again, a mistake.

One she had sworn not to repeat.

Eve swallowed and kept her place with effort. She flashed another brisk, efficient, I-have-everything-completely-under-control smile. "I didn't know you as well then."

He folded his arms, studying her. "So you don't think I made a mistake?"

"No, of course I don't think you made a mistake with this house." Eve was now seeing what he had all along, how it would look once it was redone and Derek and his daughter were in residence. "Why?" She paused, alarm bells sounding. "Are you having a case of buyer's remorse?"

He chuckled and shook his head. "When I make a decision, that's it, as far as I'm concerned. The problem is, my mother thinks I make them too quickly."

Aware that her knees were suddenly feeling a little shaky, Eve took the only available seat—on the window bench next to him. She dropped her gaze to the fine fabric of his suit trousers and swallowed again. "And you don't think that is the case."

Derek shifted slightly, his knee almost touching her thigh. "Probably because I wasn't always like this." He settled back in the deep window well and loosened the knot of his tie, tugged it down an inch. Undid the first button of his shirt. "I didn't always go with my gut instincts."

Trying not to think what he would look like with that shirt off, Eve pushed the thought away and asked, "What were you like?"

His lips twisting ruefully, he admitted, "Analytical to a fault. It's what got me into my first marriage, which was, in hindsight, the biggest mistake of my life." Abruptly, the distant brooding look was back on his face. Sorrow and regret crept into his low tone. "The only good thing about it was Tiffany. Had I not married Carleen, I wouldn't have my daughter."

Able to see he needed comforting the same way she had the night her mother had checked herself out of the hospital, Eve reached over and squeezed Derek's hand. "You're very lucky to have her. She is such a beautiful child. Always a good way to look at it."

He brought his other hand around to cover hers, and squeezed slightly, inundating her with his warmth and strength. Then, restive again, he stood and began to pace. Finally, he pivoted to face her and admitted gruffly, "When it came to choosing a mate the first time around, I ignored my instincts, which told me that although I liked Carleen very much, and we were great friends, we never had the physical passion we should have had." He let out a long, slow breath. "And I know now you should never marry someone you aren't completely wild about."

"So it's not a mistake you intend to make again."

Derek slid Eve a pointed look and shook his head. "If and when I marry again, it will be because I know for certain that the two of us have what it takes to grow old together."

She stood, too, realizing they had lingered for far too long. She felt Derek's eyes on her as she straightened her skirt and walked toward the door on legs that felt shaky again. "You agree with my position, I take it?" he drawled.

Eve nodded and moved past him toward the stairs. Hand on the rail, she made her way down to the first floor. "I think marriage is serious business. To be successful, you have to be one-hundred-percent sure it's the right thing."

Derek was close behind her. "We're on the same page, then."

She paused at the newel post in the foyer. "Apparently."

Another silence fell, more companionable this time. They walked through the downstairs, switching off lights here and there, closing more blinds. "But back to business," he said, when at last they had finished and were about to head for the front door. "Now that we've concluded ours, there really is nothing stopping us from moving on."

There was something new in his voice. Something that had an exciting ring to it. Eve's throat grew dry and tight. "Moving on how?" she rasped.

He smiled, sexy and self-assured. "By having that first date."

"A date," she repeated, achingly aware of how good it felt to be flirting with Derek, without the specter of business between them. Too good, if she was honest....

He gently cupped her shoulders with his big palms, keeping her in front of him when she would have run. "You know," he explained in a deadpan tone. "A social occasion between two people that usually is romantic in nature."

Pretending she wasn't totally thrilled with the very idea, Eve nodded with mock gravity. Damned if he didn't have the most mesmerizing eyes. And smile. Darn it if she didn't like—and lust after— nearly everything about him. "Ah," she quipped. "That kind of date."

"Yes." He stepped nearer, standing so close she could feel the heat of his body, inhale his cologne and see the sudden intensity in his eyes. "Would you like to go on one with me?"

More than he knew. But wary of rushing headlong into anything only for them to both regret it a few weeks from now, Eve held up her index finger and extricated herself from his grip. Then she walked a short distance away, pulled her phone from her purse and quickly accessed her calendar.

Aware of his eyes lingering on her, she said, "Sure. Just let me check my schedule." Flushing slightly, she scrolled through a host of open Friday and Saturday nights, finally settling on a date several weeks away. That would pretty much guarantee whatever fire they had flickering between them now would be completely cooled off. "How about Thursday, January 15?" she asked finally.

Derek tilted his head slightly to one side. "Don't you mean December?"

Eve shook her head, doing her best to hold her own with this sexy, determined man. "January."

The glimmer of hot pursuit lit his dark blue eyes. "That's all you've got open?" he probed.

Being careful to keep her screen where he couldn't see it, she scrolled some more, past many an empty evening. "Well, January 30 is available, too." She looked up, poker-faced. "At lunch."

"I'll take the fifteenth."

She should have known he wouldn't back down.

Well, she wouldn't, either. All brisk efficiency once again, Eve asked, "What time?"

"Seven-thirty."

She typed his name into the slot. "Seven-thirty it is."

Derek strolled closer. "In the meantime, should an opening arise…"

Eve slid her phone back into her pocket. "I'll be sure to let you know. But given that I'm especially busy right now, covering for my mom—" she wrinkled her nose playfully "—I doubt it will happen." *Unless, of course, I give in to the extraordinary chemistry between us. Which I won't!*

Derek gazed at her in concern. "When will Marjorie be back in the office?"

Eve recalled the kindness he had shown her mother, a fact that only deepened her attraction. "Early January."

He smiled in relief, apparently as glad to hear the news as she had been. "When you see her, give her my best."

"I will," Eve promised.

"In the meantime, we both have to get back to work." Reluctantly, Derek let Eve go. They said a cordial good-bye. He went off to listen to more proposals from hopeful entrepreneurs in the tech industry.

Eve devoted the rest of the afternoon to preparing another list of architecturally interesting homes to scope out in case the Santiago Florres house that Red Bloom was flying in from Houston to see didn't work out.

After that task was finally done, she spent the evening with her mother. Yet busy as she was, Derek was never far from her thoughts. She couldn't help but wonder if he was thinking of her, too.

On Thursday, she went to see two potential clients who were planning to list their homes in the first quarter of the next year. Eve toured the properties and spoke with the owners about their expectations, then promised to get back to them with a suggested listing price by the end of the week.

She was just heading back to the office when her phone rang again. It was a text message from Derek. Ignoring the little thrill that went through her—it had only been twenty-four hours, and she had missed him more than she liked to admit—she took a deep breath and scanned the text. It said simply: Meet me at my house? Problem with the HVAC. I could use your advice.

Chapter Six

"Why did you text the Realtor?" Harvey Jefferson, the HVAC installer, asked Derek.

Why indeed, Derek thought. Except that he was jumping at just the thought of seeing Eve again…and his ego told him she was probably feeling the same way, even if she was too cautious and too stubborn to admit it.

"Are you sure Eve even wants to be involved in this?" Harvey continued with a beleaguered frown. "I mean, technically—"

Derek knew where the installer was going. "The sale is complete. Her job as a Realtor is done."

Harvey nodded.

"I'd like Eve's opinion." *And I'd really like to see her again, even if it is only about business.* An answering text came through. "We're in luck." Derek grinned at Harvey, happy his hunch had paid off. "She's on her way." Even though—technically—she did not have to be.

Ten minutes later, Eve showed up, looking every bit the polished professional in a tweed jacket, red silk blouse, trim black skirt and heels. With her golden-brown hair glinting in the winter sunshine as she emerged from her Mercedes, Derek decided she was gorgeous enough to stop traffic.

Feeling a pang of guilt for objectifying her that way, he tore his eyes from her spectacular legs as she moved up the sidewalk.

With a concerned look on her face, she crossed the weed-choked lawn to where he and his contractor were standing next to the dual units on the rear wall. Like everything else, the big metal HVACs were rusty and out-of-date. Both were on and making hideous grinding noises.

Eve glanced cautiously at the whirling fans inside the units. Then at the two big boxes beyond, containing brand-new state-of-the-art machines waiting to be installed. "Hey, fellas, what's up?"

Harvey Jefferson, the HVAC installer, winced. "I'd rather just show you both." He motioned them inside, then led them through the mass of workers tearing up carpeting and damaged flooring, to the kitchen. The burly man stopped beneath a vent in the ceiling and lifted a hand. "Feel anything?"

Eve and Derek both raised their hands. Their glances met. "Nothing," they murmured in unison.

Still grimacing, Harvey led them to the guest bath. "Feel anything here?"

Eve and Derek stood under the vent. It was faint, Derek thought, but he could feel a flow of air. So could Eve.

"Let's try the family room," the contractor suggested.

There, small, staticky bursts of air were coming out of the vents, although the slats in the grates were wide open.

"Do you think something might be blocking it?" Derek asked.

"Like a squirrel nest?" Eve interjected.

Derek looked at her.

She gestured matter-of-factly. "It happens in houses that have been untended for a long time. Our furry friends decide to move right in."

Derek chuckled at her wry tone. He liked a woman who could not only take the most challenging situations in stride, but joke about them.

The HVAC guy was not laughing, however. "I only wish it was that simple," Harvey muttered. He led them over to a ladder, beneath where an air duct grill had been removed. He took a mirror and a flashlight out of his shirt pocket. "It's going to be kind of hard to see, but if you climb up the ladder and look that way…" He pointed in the direction of the HVAC units outside the house.

Derek gestured for Eve to go first.

She started to do so, then stopped, removed her black suede pumps and handed them to Derek. In stocking feet, she climbed the ladder. Squinting, she looked where the contractor had pointed. "I don't… Ohhh." Her voice turned as grim as her expression as she glanced down at the contractor. After inching back down the ladder, she wordlessly exchanged the flashlight and mirror for her shoes.

Derek offered his forearm in support as she slipped her heels back on. Despite the decidedly unromantic circumstances, he couldn't help liking the way it felt to have her leaning on him, even for a second or two. Then, aware that neither Harvey nor Eve wanted to be the bearer of bad news, he went up the ladder and looked around. It took him a moment to figure out what was what, but as his eyes adjusted to the dim lighting, he eventually saw the problem, too. "The ductwork inside the walls is collapsing." And where it wasn't collapsing, it seemed to be almost crumbling to bits.

Big sighs and more grave looks were exchanged between Eve and the contractor.

Derek came back down the ladder. "What does this mean?" Obviously, something bad. Harvey winced as if bracing himself for an angry reaction. "There's no other way to say it. All the ductwork is going to have to be replaced. Otherwise, there's no point to putting in new units. And the only way to get at it is to cut through the drywall and the ceilings. That will take time."

Derek could only imagine. His dream of having Tiffany in their new home in time to celebrate the Christmas holiday began to fade. "How much time?" he asked grimly.

Again, Harvey seemed to brace himself. "Two, three more days than what we figured."

Eve added, "The interior painting can't be started until they're done and the drywall is repaired or replaced."

And every day counted. Derek turned to Eve, knowing she would have a good overview. "How many more issues like this can we expect?"

She kept her gaze locked with his and replied with a frankness he admired, "I don't know. If you'd opted to have an inspection, we'd have some idea."

But he hadn't opted for one. Hadn't wanted to take the time to get one done, or let the results in any way infringe on his purchase of the property.

Derek silently racked his brain for a solution that would keep them on schedule. "Can your crews work around the clock if I pay double time?"

Eve tensed and stepped in. "There is a city ordinance preventing that. And even if there weren't, Derek, it'd be a bad idea to disturb your neighbors or their kids with construction when they're trying to sleep. Never mind disrupt the horse-drawn carriage tours of the holiday light displays."

Derek hadn't thought of that. He had simply been focused on his goal.

Harvey added, "The best we can do is work seven days a week with as many guys as I can round up. And have the other contractors do the same."

"We'll find a way to have you and Tiffany in your new home by Christmas," Eve promised.

Derek hoped so. Failing in his marriage was one thing; failing his child was something else entirely. This was Tiffany's first Christmas with him, as a divorced single dad. He did not want her spending it in a hotel.

"How upset was Derek McCabe?" Marjorie asked later that afternoon, after Eve had filled her in.

Eve took a seat next to her in the solarium on the roof of the hospital annex. Glad Marjorie was well enough now to handle small amounts of stress, she paused.

"It was hard to tell." Sometimes she was able to read Derek like a book. At others, she hadn't a clue. And when he had departed he had seemed unusually quiet and more brooding than she had ever seen him, even during that frustrating house-hunting search that had repeatedly left him empty-handed.

Marjorie put down the novel she had been reading when Eve arrived for her daily visit. Another first. Before her heart attack her mom had never taken time for leisure reading. Or any other hobby or relaxing activity. It had been nothing but work, work, work for Marjorie.

"But you suspect he was unhappy," the older woman said.

Sighing wearily, Eve sipped some of the decaf peppermint tea she had brought them from the hospital cafeteria. "Wouldn't you be if you had news like that?" She searched her mother's face, heartened to see she was looking a little less pale and drawn every day now. "Especially because we don't know what else could go wrong with the house. I mean, for all we know, it could be a real money pit."

Marjorie reached for her teacup. "Fortunately, Derek is a man of means and steely determination."

Aware what a good judge of character her mother was, Eve nodded. "He is that."

"And it was his decision not to have an inspection. I don't think he'll blame you for that."

"You're right. He isn't the kind of man to push responsibility for his actions off on someone else."

Both women smiled.

"But you're wise to be concerned," Eve's mom continued. "When a buyer is unhappy with the home they've purchased, the Realtor involved invariably ends up taking the blame."

"I've done everything I can do to help when it comes to Harvey Jefferson and the other contractors," Eve said. And though she knew she was becoming too personally involved, she couldn't help it. She had promised a client he would be able to spend the holiday with his baby girl in their new home. It was a promise neither she nor Derek had taken lightly. A promise that, if broken, would have lasting repercussions.

"Then there's only one thing left to do," Marjorie advised with a maternal pat on the forearm.

Eve grinned, recalling the business training her mother had given her. "The triage approach. Identify the problem, come up with a solution and apply it."

Marjorie beamed with pride. "Exactly! Glad to see you were paying attention, after all."

Suddenly eager to put her plan into action, Eve stood and kissed her on her cheek. "Thanks, Mom. I knew you'd have the answer."

And the answer, Eve thought, was finding Derek, and making sure that their relationship, business and otherwise, was still okay.

AN HOUR LATER, Eve arrived at Derek's hotel, determined to not only bring tidings of good cheer, but find out if anything else was wrong that he had yet to tell her about. If there was, she was resolved to do what she could to help him rectify the situation.

I have something for you and Tiffany, she texted him. Shall I leave it at the front desk?

He texted back, It would be better if you brought it up.

Well, that was a good sign, wasn't it? Eve took the elevator to his floor, determined to help him start celebrating the holiday season more fully.

Derek was waiting for her when she stepped off with overflowing shopping bags in both hands. She smiled at him, then at the baby girl cuddled in his arms. Tiffany's cute little face was red, her lower lip trembling, her cheeks wet with tears.

Derek shot Eve a grateful glance. He looked so harried and distraught that her heart went out to him.

"You couldn't have come at a better time." Tiffany still in his arms, Derek opened the door and ushered Eve into his suite.

She set her bags down, gifts momentarily forgotten. "What's going on?" she asked.

Derek pursed his lips in concern. "She wants her *m-o-m-m-y*."

Oh, dear.

Tiffany's lower lip thrust even farther out. Abruptly, she started to cry again. "Mommy. Mommy. Mommy…"

Derek murmured, "It's all right, honey," and patted her back consolingly. To no avail. Tiffany wailed on, clearly miserable, and Eve's heart went out to the child, as well. This was the part of divorce and split custody that no one wanted to talk about.

"What can I do?" Eve whispered.

Before Derek could reply, Tiffany looked at her, said "Mommy!" again and stretched out her arms. After shifting her weight, she lurched unexpectedly toward Eve. Derek made sure she had caught his little girl before letting her go. Then he stepped back, clearly exhausted and grateful for the emotional backup, while Eve cuddled the infant close.

"Mommy!" Tiffany squealed, happier now. With a giggle, she wound her hands in Eve's hair and tugged.

Derek made a face, as if knowing how uncomfortable that must be, and stepped in to try and extricate the tiny fists. While he worked at it gently, the warmth of his body so close by flooded Eve's.

"It's a new thing, apparently." Derek untangled one fist, only to have Tiffany reach again for Eve's mane when he went to work on the other.

Still untangling carefully, Derek continued, "It's been going on the past two days. Whenever Carleen and Craig are both there, Tiffany is fine. But if Craig leaves, Tiffany cries for *d-a-d-d-y*. And now she's started doing it with me. If Carleen isn't here, or it would seem, you, she wants an *m-o-m-m-y*."

"Or, in other words, an adult female, and a male presence."

"Right." Derek gave up on extricating Tiffany's hands and went to get two toys. He held them out in front of his daughter. Tiffany thought about it for a moment, then let go of Eve's hair so she could reach for them.

With Eve more comfortable, Derek continued with what he'd been saying. "Carlene talked to Tiffany's pediatrician—Dr. Maydew—and she said it's no wonder Tiffany's confused, with the recent moves, in addition to growing up in a split-custody arrangement. Dr. Maydew said Tiffany is old enough to be aware of her surroundings, and is just reacting to being in a hotel one moment, Carleen and Craig's huge new house the next...."

Eve gazed down at the sweet little girl in her arms, wishing there was something she could say or do to help.

"Eventually, the pediatrician said, Tiffany will be fine wherever she is, as long as she's with people who love her. But right now, she just wants what every child wants."

"A mommy and a daddy and a secure place to call home," Eve guessed, privately sharing Derek's worry and anxiety. This had to be tough.

Well, she'd been right about one thing at least, Eve thought. It hadn't been just the failing HVAC ductwork that had been bothering Derek today.

Glad she had come, she bounced the baby girl in her arms, noting that the brooding look was back in Derek's eyes. "Well, then it's a good thing I brought a distraction," she said cheerfully, smiling when Tiffany started wiggling, signaling she wanted down.

Eve set the toddler gently on the floor, and she scampered off in the direction of the shopping bags.

Derek inclined his head. "What's all that?"

Eve grinned and sashayed forward. "You'll see," she promised with a wink.

With Derek and his little girl watching intently, she opened the first oversize bag and pulled out a box. Inside was a two-foot-tall artificial Christmas tree with battery-run lights. Made to sit atop a table or desk, it added instant holiday cheer to the otherwise bland hotel room.

With Derek's help, she drew it out of the box. "Where do you want it?"

He looked around the living area of his two-bedroom suite. "On the bar, I think. Out of reach, but where she can see it."

Eve set it there, then went back to her bags and reached for one containing tissue-wrapped presents. "This is for Tiffany. It's meant for a baby's first Christmas tree."

Derek sat down on the sofa with his daughter snuggled beside him. He let Tiffany unwrap the tissue paper and pull out several cloth ornaments. The little girl chortled when she saw the Santa and Mrs. Claus. She giggled at the reindeer with its bright red nose, and smiled at the gingham candy canes and miniature teddy bears.

"Now she's happy," Derek murmured in a deep voice.

Eve draped the bottom of the little evergreen with a quilted skirt embroidered with the words *Merry Christmas, Everyone!*

Finished, she turned back to him, a little embarrassed that she had let herself get so into this. "I know it's not the same as being in your house right now," she told him soberly, ordering herself to keep at least some emotional distance. She pulled two stockings out of the bag. One embroidered with Derek's name, the other with Tiffany's. Eve hung them side by side on the doorknobs of the tall armoire housing the television set. Again, both were safely out of reach of the toddler. "But hopefully, this will add a little touch of Christmas to your world in the meantime."

"Thank you," Derek said in a voice that was husky and soft, and so tender it brought forth an answering well of warmth in Eve.

Grinning, Tiffany scooted toward the edge of the sofa. Once she'd climbed down onto the floor, she toddled around, a stuffed ornament in each little hand. Jabbering nonstop, she placed the ornaments here and there and everywhere, beaming all the while.

Derek sat watching, relaxed and content. He exhaled again, then turned and locked eyes with Eve. "This was just what we needed. Thank you, Eve."

Glad she'd acted on instinct instead of letting her usual reserve rule her, she smiled back. "You're welcome." Then, knowing it was time she left before she was tempted to do anything else "instinctive," she looked around for her purse.

Once again, Derek was beside her, his hand on her arm. "Don't go," he said in a gently compelling voice. "Stay and have dinner here tonight."

As IT TURNED out, Tiffany had already eaten. She just needed her pajamas, bedtime bottle and story. And she wanted them from Eve, not Derek.

Everything in Eve that wanted to be a mother was eager to participate. But wary of jumping in even deeper into a situation that could easily leave her with a broken heart, she hesitated. "Should we? Because I'm not usually going to be here with the two of you."

Derek sat down beside Eve with Tiffany on his lap.

The little girl grabbed a fistful of each of their clothes, trying to bring them closer together. Derek obliged by scooting over until the side of his body touched Eve's. "Who knows what tomorrow will bring? All I know is she's happy to have both of us with her, so I think we should just go with that."

Because if they didn't, Eve knew, Tiffany was likely to start crying again for a mommy. It had been hard enough earlier, seeing her so upset.

"You're the expert." Eve smiled down at Tiffany, who crawled off Derek's lap and onto hers. Looking utterly content, the little girl leaned her head against Eve's chest and propped her pajama-clad feet on Derek's lap. Grinning and babbling, she held her bottle with one hand, looking happily from one adult to the other as she drank.

By the time she'd drained the bottle, her eyes were closing. And by the time Derek finished reading the story about the bear who accidentally slept through Christmas, she was sound asleep.

"Now for the really tricky part," Derek whispered, easing the empty baby bottle out of his daughter's hand. "Getting her into bed without waking her."

Eve held her breath as he stood, leaned over and slipped his hands between Tiffany's relaxed form and Eve's chest. Oblivious to the immediate tingling in her body that resulted, he started to lift his daughter.

The pout on the little one's face was back.

Derek waited, not moving, and Eve barely breathed, for another minute, then two.

Tiffany relaxed back into sleep.

Slowly, carefully, Derek lifted her, shifted her gently, then carried her into the adjacent bedroom where her crib was set up.

Aching with a similar need to be held and cared for, Eve stood and tried to calm her racing heart. Her taut nipples, her body's awareness, meant nothing, she told herself. But when Derek came back to her, she could see that it did.

He was grateful. Gratitude in that man-who-has-just-been-rescued-by-an-intuitive-woman kind of way. Which was, Eve realized with no small amount of irony, not what she wanted from him at all.

"So how about that dinner?" Derek said, watching the conflicting mix of wistfulness and hesitation cross Eve's face. He sensed she was as attracted to him as he was to her, yet determined not to act on the chemistry again, too. Feeling a little frustrated about it, as well as the fact that he hadn't been able to comfort his child on his own, yet deeply grateful for Eve's intervention, he walked toward her with a casual smile and handed her a leather-bound menu. "It seems I owe you whatever room service can provide."

Eve glanced at her watch, noting that it was after eight. "Thanks," she said politely, "but I really should go."

"Sure?" Derek asked, oddly disappointed that she didn't seem to think they should be enjoying these interactions as much as they actually were. He searched her face, looking for a way to persuade her. "It doesn't have to be a date."

A furrow formed along the bridge of her nose. "But you'd like it to be."

He took a deep breath and stuffed his hands in the

pockets of his slacks, aware it wasn't like him to get attached to a woman so quickly, never mind one as gorgeous as Eve. And she *was* gorgeous tonight, with her hair down, her lips soft and bare, the light of awareness shimmering in her pretty amber eyes.

Derek shrugged and continued frankly, "I'm not going to pretend I don't want to spend time with you." *Man-and-woman time. The kind we're not likely to forget.*

She hitched in an uneven breath, even as she quirked her lips in a sassy smile. "At least we cleared that up," she joked.

He let his gaze drift over her, noting the imprint of her nipples beneath her blouse. "You don't want me to be honest?"

A turbulent light came into her eyes and she stepped away. "I don't want you to move so fast."

Derek edged closer anyway. He knew she was wary at heart. He also knew that wariness was keeping her from getting really close to anyone. "Why did you come over here tonight, then—if not to further our...whatever you'd like to call this?"

She angled her head to one side, as if studying him that way would give her greater insight into what was going on inside him. Silky hair fell across her shoulders, onto her breast. "I didn't want you to be an unhappy former client," she said softly.

Wishing he didn't want to take her to bed quite so much, he drawled, "Bad for business?"

She smiled as the flirtatious mood between them intensified. "Very, as it happens."

Derek cupped her shoulders between his palms. "You know what I think?"

Her tongue came out to briefly wet her lips. "I'm not

sure I want to know," she told him hoarsely, but, to his satisfaction, didn't move away.

Feeling the pressure building at the front of his jeans, he noted with a wink, "I think the Christmas tree and the trimmings were just an excuse to be with me again."

She blushed. "You've got no shortage of ego."

"No shortage of desire," Derek corrected, glad the interest wasn't one-sided. He wrapped his arms around her and brought her closer still. Eve caught her breath but didn't move away. Her nipples were taut, her knees trembling slightly.

Derek lowered his head, aware he wasn't the only one who was so turned on he could barely breathe. "Kiss me," he whispered, even more softly, "and tell me you don't feel the same."

Chapter Seven

Eve wanted to tell Derek she didn't desire him. She wanted to tell him she didn't want him to pull her against him. But the moment his lips found hers, all rational thought dissipated. Need entered the picture, and it was a yearning that refused to subside. When Derek finally lifted his head, the question she knew was coming glimmered in his beautiful blue eyes: Was this what she wanted? Because if not, they both knew they needed to stop. *Now.*

Eve forced herself to be practical. And practicality told her she would not be able to stop thinking about him like this unless she answered some very fundamental questions. Such as, was making love to Derek going to be as heavenly as merely kissing him?

Aware that if he had any doubts, he sure wasn't showing them, she hitched in a tremulous breath. "Normally I am not into one-night stands, but we need to get each other out of our systems."

A corner of his mouth lifted in a sexy smile. He tucked a strand of hair behind her ear. "We need something, all right."

And Eve knew exactly what that was.

She'd been wondering what gift to get herself. At first, way back in the beginning, she'd decided it would be not working with him. Now, she wanted something different. Still holding his devastating gaze, she flashed a smile. "It *is* Christmas…."

His eyes crinkled at the corners, the idea of making love to each other evidently as enthralling to him as it was to her. She lifted her face to his and teased, "What's Christmas without at least one gift to ourselves?"

"Ah." He nuzzled her neck, then danced her backward toward the bedroom he'd been using as an office. "A woman after my own heart."

He let her go just long enough to gather all the folders and the computer, and stack them on the chair. Eve shrugged out of her red cashmere cardigan and toed off her black suede heels. "Just so you know, this one time is all it will be."

He unbuttoned his shirt. "I hear you."

Eve helped him remove it and then his T-shirt. His chest was sleek with satiny muscles, and a dusting of hair that arrowed down to his navel and disappeared into the waistband of his trousers. Damn, but he was beautiful. Inside and out. Forcing herself to concentrate only on the physical, she ran her hands over the warmth of his skin, appreciating the masculine strength. "But you don't believe me."

Derek let her explore to her heart's content. "I think you mean it now." He eased down the zipper at the back of her black-and-red sheath dress.

"What you'll want after I do this…" The fine wool fabric fell over her hips and puddled on the floor at her feet. He bent to kiss the exposed arch of her throat, and then paused to admire the nipples protruding through the semi-sheer fabric of her red bra. "And this…" His lips dropped to her breast.

"And this…"

She trembled as her bra came off.

"...may be something else entirely." His lips found the aching crowns, the valley between, the sensitive uppermost curves.

Eve closed her eyes, luxuriating in the feel of his tongue making lazy designs on her skin. She had never felt more beautiful than she did at that moment.

The next thing she knew, her black tights were being peeled off. Then her sheer red panties.

Moments later, Derek joined her, naked, between the sheets.

Eve had thought if she accepted her desire, and celebrated it freely, she would be able to control her reaction to him. She hadn't banked on how it would feel having his bare form pressed up against hers. She hadn't counted on the abundance of his masculinity or the skill with which he took her in his arms and made a leisurely tour of her entire body. Starting with her lips, then her throat and breasts, before moving lower still, across the quivery plane of her abdomen to the inside of her thighs. She arched as he found the most sensitive part of her, and caught his head in her hands.

And then all was lost in the glorious possession of his lips and caresses, and the tenderness he bestowed.

Satisfaction roared through Derek as Eve shuddered and fell apart in his hands. He waited until her trembling subsided, then moved up over her and slid between her thighs, his need to make her his stronger than ever. Clasping her against him, he kissed her hard and long, soft and deep, and every way in between. He kissed her until she moaned, her hands moving over him, finding him every bit as ready for more as she was. Their eyes locked again, and the sound of their ragged breathing filled the room.

"Now?" he whispered, touching her yet again.

"Now." Eve arched, and he slid all the way home. She was as hot, silky and wet as he had imagined. Her lips found his and her body closed around him, demanding, pleading, urging him on. They moved in perfect union, again and again, until Derek was lost in the sweet essence that was Eve. And suddenly, for him, life was better than it had been in a long, long time.

"STAY."

With a sheet draped loosely around her, Eve bent to retrieve her clothes.

Her body might be sated, but her emotions were in tatters. "I can't."

Derek lay on his side, all six feet three inches of him sprawled out across the queen-size bed. Unlike her, he found no need to cover up, now that their first—and only—lovemaking session had ended.

Flushing, Eve turned her glance from the part of him that indicated he was as ready for more as she secretly was.

She steeled herself against the desire still roaring through her. "I've got two important meetings tomorrow." Pretending an ease she couldn't begin to feel, she slipped into the bathroom and put on her bra and panties. "The first is with a client from Houston, who collects interesting houses the way others amass fine art."

Realizing she had yet to locate her tights, Eve came back into the bedroom. Feeling suddenly self-conscious in her red satin-and-lace undergarments, she circled the bed where Derek lay watching her, a mixture of delight and satisfaction in his gaze. "He's interested in one designed by Santiago Florres."

"The Texas architect who builds homes like ultra-modern mazes."

"Right." Spying her tights at last, Eve snatched them off the floor and started putting them on. "My mother has been courting this investor forever. He's coming to town to look at a property tomorrow. I have to pick him up at Love Field in the afternoon." Nearly dressed, she stepped into her sheath. "In the morning, I have to meet with Flash Lefleur—"

Lazily, Derek stood and tugged on his boxer-briefs, still listening to her intently. "The hockey player who was traded to Montreal last summer."

The snug-fitting cotton highlighted the sensual contours of his generous physique in a way that made Eve want to undress him all over again. Forcing herself to remain as strong and disciplined as she needed to be, she smiled. "Yes. I listed his condo almost five months ago. But Flash has refused to do the things required to actually sell it. Luckily, he's going to be in town for tomorrow night's game, and agreed to meet with me while he's in Dallas…."

Trying to keep her mind from veering into forbidden territory, she cleared her throat, then continued. "Because there has been so little interest in the property despite its stellar location, I'm hoping to talk sense into Flash at long last. But I only have a few minutes, after his morning practice wraps up, to do it." She located her pumps and slipped into them.

Derek put on his pants and then his shirt, unabashed admiration in his eyes. "If Lefleur's smart, he'll listen to you. You know your stuff."

Aware that Derek could easily make her forget everything but making love to him again, Eve drew in a jerky breath. She held him off with a roll of her eyes and a look that would have sent a lesser man running for the exit. "Flattery will get you absolutely—"

"Where I want to go?" With a teasing smile, he pulled her against him. His eyes mirrored everything she felt, and the knowledge was staggering. So tender, so yearning… It would be so easy to fall in love with him.

Too easy. Eve gulped and did her best to keep her vulnerable heart in check. "The sex was great, Derek." Pretending to be a lot more casual about all this than she was, she splayed her hands across his hard chest.

His heart thudded heavily beneath her palms. Ignoring her efforts to keep him at bay, he playfully nuzzled the side of her neck, finding the nerve endings just beneath her ear. He kissed her again, in a way no one else ever had. Or likely ever would.

Finally, he drew back, his eyes meeting hers. "No argument there," he said softly. "It was spectacular for me, too."

Eve wet her lips. "But I meant what I said about this being a make-love-once-and-we're-done affair."

His grin widened. "I know."

She willed her knees to vanquish their trembling. "Then…?"

His blue eyes twinkled. "Even so, a Texas gentleman never ends an evening without a proper good-night."

Eve should have seen the last kiss coming. Should have seen a lot of things coming. Like the fact that, since Derek was the kind of man who went after what he wanted with no holds barred, he wasn't likely to end their one-and-only encounter without a kiss.

And not just any kiss, but one that made another chink in the wall around her heart, and nearly drove her to her knees. When he finally lifted his lips, she was a puddle of desire once again.

DEREK WALKED EVE to the door, said a casual goodbye and watched her slip away. He knew she had told him that this was a one-time event. But he didn't believe that would be the case.

For starters, she wasn't the kind of woman who could make love without feelings being involved, even though she had clearly tried her best to do so. Second, even though she didn't want to get emotionally involved, they already were. The fact that they couldn't seem to stay away from each other, and the hot, reckless way they'd just made love, proved just how interlinked their lives were becoming.

Getting Eve to admit that, however, was not going to be easy.

Not only was she one of the most independent and elusive women he had ever met, she was cautious to a fault. Part of it likely had to do with the way she and her mom had been abandoned by her wealthy, well-connected father. The rest was because she had gotten involved with the wrong guy for the wrong reasons before, and consequently was scared of laying her heart on the line.

Derek understood that, but he wasn't willing to throw away the best thing he'd ever had, either.

The kind of connection he and Eve had found in each other was a rare occurrence.

So he would do whatever it took to make sure they continued to build on that connection. And have faith that patience and understanding would ultimately bring them the happiness they both deserved.

HER TENSE BUT ultimately productive meeting with Flash Lefleur behind her, Eve was at the airport the next afternoon, awaiting the arrival of Red Bloom's private jet, when a text from Derek came in. Need advice re house. Free to meet tonight?

Eve contemplated the message, her heart racing. This was the point where she should be gently but determinedly extricating herself from her former client, to concentrate more fully on her current ones. Yet she couldn't bring herself to do so, any more than she had been able to tear herself from his arms before they'd made love and satisfied their mutual curiosity once and for all, the night before.

She bit her lip, still thinking. After further deliberation, she typed, May still be tied up with client tonight. Particularly if things went as well as she hoped with the Houston oilman and home collector. Can someone else in the office help you? She hit Send.

Thirty seconds later, Derek replied, Prefer you. Will check with you later.

Which, Eve thought as she studied the screen, left a lot of options open. They could end up spending another evening together. Or be involved in something that was strictly business. Or not see each other at all. She knew what she was privately hoping for. And it wasn't the sensible route to take.

But then nothing about her involvement with Derek was sensible, she thought, sighing wistfully. And that worried her almost as much as her upcoming appointment with Red Bloom.

For her mother's sake, she really needed to make the sale.

Unfortunately, as much as Red Bloom liked the

uniquely designed contemporary home, he was not going to be reasonable.

"I can't present the owners with an offer like that," Eve protested, upon hearing what the businessman was prepared to bid. "It's only half what the property is listed for!" The owners weren't about to take a two-million-dollar loss.

Unimpressed, Bloom looked around the elegantly appointed home. Like many self-made men, the sixty-something bachelor was dressed to suit himself, in designer jeans, alligator boots and a tailored suede jacket with patches on the elbows. Freckles dotted his weathered face, and a dark brown Resistol was tipped up over his fading auburn hair. "How many bids have the current owners had?" He stroked his mustache thoughtfully.

"None," Eve conceded reluctantly. The mazelike floor plan and starkly contemporary exterior, in an area of mostly traditional homes, had seen to that. "But I believe it will sell eventually, at close to what it's priced."

Bloom clearly did not agree. He persisted curtly, "Make the offer."

Somehow managing not to sigh in frustration, Eve reached for her phone and did as her client bid.

"Well?" he said, when the round of calls had finally been completed.

"The answer is no." Unequivocally, angrily, no.

His handsome brow furrowed. "They understood that I was the one placing the bid?"

A fact that had made it all the more insulting, since Red Bloom was well known as an astute collector of unique architectural designs. Eve affirmed this with a nod. "They did."

"And they didn't even counter?"

Deliberately, she kept her manner matter-of-fact. She might not want to waste any more of her own time with Red Bloom, but in this situation she had little choice. Her mother had been courting the oilman for months, trying to get him to come to Dallas to see the Santiago Florres home that Marjorie was certain was perfect for Red's collection of eccentric properties. "Their view is that it's the asking price or above. Or nothing."

Bloom scoffed in disbelief. He took off his hat and slapped it against his thigh. "That's too bad. It would have been nice to add a Santiago Florres to my real estate portfolio."

It would have been nice, Eve thought, to get the sale on her mother's behalf. And keep Loughlin Realty firmly in the lead of the Highland Park real estate sales race. But she hadn't. And now she would have to tell her mother that disappointing news, too.

Unable to interest Bloom in looking at anything else that day or any other, Eve drove the oilman back to the airport. The two of them said a cordial goodbye, despite the fact they knew they would likely never see each other again.

Dispirited and exhausted, Eve called Sasha and her mother to let them know what had happened, then headed back to the office. And found an even bigger surprise waiting.

DEREK HAD EXPECTED Eve to be pleasantly stunned to see him waiting for her with a yuletide horse and buggy. However, he hadn't expected her to look so incredibly gorgeous after such a long day. In a cranberry wool coat, suit and heels, her hair drawn up in back, she was the epitome of sophistication.

The look she gave him, when she realized what he

was doing there, was cool, however. He moved out of earshot of the driver, as did she.

Aware they were being observed by everyone in the vicinity, especially those coming out of her office building, she repeated his invitation as if she couldn't possibly have understood him correctly. "You want to look at Christmas lights? Right now?"

He shrugged affably and kept his gaze locked with hers. He'd known even before they'd hit the sheets that Eve would regret making love prior to them really getting to know each other. He'd seduced her anyway, and now was paying the price for their mutual recklessness. Her coolness toward him would likely continue unless they took several steps back and established even more of a close personal relationship.

Knowing it was going to take a lot of persuading to get her to go out with him, he ambled close enough to take in her hyacinth perfume. "I hear yuletide carriage rides are a tradition in this neck of the woods."

She studied him, offering no clue as to what was in her heart. "It's quite a gamble, showing up with a horse and buggy." She looked him up and down and narrowed her gaze. "What if I hadn't been here?"

A fresh wave of guilt wafted through him. Figuring if Eve was going to hear it, she may as well hear it from him, Derek admitted, "Sasha told me when I called the office that you were expected shortly."

Determination stiffened Eve's slender frame. "Then she should have also told you that I had a very long day, and will probably have an even longer one tomorrow."

If ever a woman needed tender loving care, Eve was it. "Then it's a good thing I'm here with just the holiday distraction you need." He paused. "Unless…you've already taken a leisurely tour of this year's best holiday light displays?"

Briefly, a wistful look crossed her face.

Clearly, Derek thought, she hadn't.

He'd known his instinct was a good one. "It's also a nice way to wind down, make the transition from time on the job to time off," he said, adding for good measure, "Not to mention get in the spirit of the holidays."

His expression hopeful, the driver tipped his hat at them. The horse snorted and pawed the ground restlessly. Derek grinned again and all three waited for Eve to decide.

She looked them over for a long moment, then propped her hands on her hips and drawled, "Well, I guess it's either this or spend the evening saying 'Bah, humbug!'"

Everyone laughed as she finally relented.

Delighted with her response, Derek helped her up into the cozy confines of the carriage and settled beside her. The evening was chilly and damp, and a luxuriously thick velvet lap robe had been provided for extra warmth. Together, they tucked it across their laps and around their legs.

There was comfort and joy to be found, Derek realized, in just sitting cuddled together on a cold and starry December night.

The carriage swayed as the horse trotted down the avenue and turned onto a suburban street. Santa's sleigh was on one lawn. A manger, complete with animals and a baby, on another. Across the street, there was a Star of David on a roof. Cartoon characters decorated another lawn, and everywhere there were festive wreaths and Christmas trees, colored and white lights. Sometimes music accompanied the displays. All were beautiful. Some moving, some funny.

Eve studied their surroundings, quiet now, at peace. Finally, she turned to Derek, her shoulder gently nudging his. "Thanks for this," she said sincerely. "I think I needed some R & R more than I knew."

He resisted the urge to reach over and squeeze her hand. Contenting himself with a long look into her eyes, he replied softly, "You're welcome."

Another companionable silence fell. Eve took a deep breath and turned back to him, her hip and thigh briefly touching his. "When you texted today, you said you needed my advice regarding your new home."

Derek nodded, serious now, too. "Even though Tiffany and I can't move in yet, I want to go ahead and decorate the outside of the home for the holidays. But I'm not sure which direction to go."

Eve squinted as if doing some mental calculations. "And you thought you'd ask me?" she asked eventually.

He admired the soft, luscious curves of her lips, and the cute way she wrinkled her nose when she was perplexed. "You do have impeccable taste."

She lifted an eyebrow. "So do you," she acknowledged. Then she waited, as if wanting to know what was really behind his unexpected request.

Derek knew he could make something up—and eventually give her further reason to want to keep him at arm's length. Or he could be honest. "Okay," he admitted with a smile. "It's just an excuse to spend time with you."

She studied him, her eyes taking on a turbulent sheen. "You thought it wouldn't happen any other way?"

Derek sobered. "Not as fast as I'd like it to happen, anyway."

She peered at him through a fringe of thick golden-brown lashes, smiling briefly as she asked, "Does anyone ever say no to you?"

She seemed to think, erroneously, that this went back to him being part of one of the most powerful clans of Texas. "That's not really the issue." It had nothing to do with him being a McCabe. "The issue is, do I ever say yes."

Eve shifted on the carriage seat again. "What do you mean?"

Ignoring the heat her brief, accidental touch generated, Derek forced himself to focus on his reply, not on how good she felt whenever she pressed up against him.

"At work, as a venture capitalist, I'm constantly sifting through proposals and hearing pitches from start-up businesses," he explained. "I turn down ninety-nine for every one that I fund, because they're just not ready for prime time, so to speak, or the idea is terminally flawed in some way."

A mixture of understanding and compassion lit her smile. She seemed to realize what so few others did—how much he hated being the bad guy in a situation. "So you're always saying no," she guessed, with no small trace of irony.

"In my business life," Derek specified. "Which is why, in my private life, I want to say yes as often as possible."

She gave an encouraging nod, as if that made sense to her, so he reached over and took her hand. "I'd think you would want to say yes a little more often, too."

"When it comes to you," Eve returned softly, looking down at their entwined fingers, "I do." After a moment, she withdrew her hand. "But that doesn't mean we *should,* Derek."

Clearly, he thought with a frustrated sigh, he had a lot more convincing to do. But he'd get there. When he wanted something as much as he wanted to be with Eve, he always did.

Chapter Eight

"So what do you think?" Derek asked, a half mile of beautifully decked out houses later. "What kind of decorations should I go for?" There was another manger on one lawn, a menorah several houses later and a Charlie Brown Christmas display at the end of the block.

The truth was, Eve didn't know him well enough yet to say. Wishing he didn't look so handsome in his cashmere coat and scarf, or that she still didn't want him quite so much, she demurred, "You could always call your designer."

He watched her adjust the velvet lap robe. "That would take all the fun out of it."

She fought the urge to cuddle against him. "True."

He sat back and draped his arm across the top of the seat, seemingly content to just be there with her. In a low, gravelly voice that sent prickles across her skin, he said, "The only thing I know for sure is that it should be something that would delight Tiffany."

Unable to help herself, Eve shifted to better see his face. "Well, there you go," she teased in a soft, sultry voice.

"But," Derek said, "in that realm, as we have seen, there are a lot of choices." Everything from Sesame Street characters to teddy bears and reindeer.

Curious, she asked, "Do you want her to believe in Santa?"

He nodded. "Carleen and I both do."

It was nice, the way he and his ex worked together to co-parent their child. Eve wished there was more of that in divorced couples. Certainly her own experience, with her mother and father detesting each other, had been less than ideal.

Aware that Derek was waiting for her reaction, Eve said, "Then there you go. Something to do with Santa and his workshop would be perfect."

Derek radiated enthusiasm. "Next question. Where do I get the stuff?"

Glad for something else to focus on aside from the dashing man beside her, Eve opened up her bag and whipped out her phone. She scrolled through several options, paused to type another more specific query, then finally came up with a list of choices. "I would recommend this place." She pointed to a popular home improvement store.

Derek glanced at his watch. "How late are they open?"

She checked the posted hours. "Until ten o'clock."

"Which means we could go now," he suggested.

For a second, Eve was tempted, but then she shook her head. "I have a big day tomorrow."

"I understand."

Moments later the carriage arrived back at Eve's office. Derek climbed down and helped her to the ground. A little sad that their time together was over, she looked up at him. "But good luck." She reached out and squeezed his hand. "I'll be thinking of you."

"And I," Eve thought she heard Derek murmur as she walked away, "will be dreaming of you."

DEREK WENT TO the hardware superstore that night, then recruited two of his brothers and his sister-in-law to help put up the decorations on Saturday morning.

"You're certainly in a cheerful mood, considering what you're dealing with in there." Derek's older brother, Grady, pointed to the crowd of contractors working on the interior of his newly purchased home.

Grady's wife, Alexis, was unraveling several outdoor extension cords. Above the sounds of hammers and saws, and vehicle doors being slammed, she called, "It's because there's a woman in his life."

Grady turned to his wife, the love he felt for her shining in his eyes. He ignored the whine of a power saw coming from the open garage. "How do you know?"

"Easy." Alexis pulled out a set of thin metal stakes and unboxed those, too. With all the authority of a professional matchmaker, she stated, "I haven't seen Derek smile the way he has today, ever. And no house, no matter how much potential it has, will ever light up any Mc-Cabe male's face like that. That kind of smile, my dear husband, comes from falling head over heels in love."

Squirming, Derek averted his gaze. He wasn't in love. *Yet.* It was way too soon for that. He was head over heels in lust. And so was Eve, if the way she had kissed him and made love to him was any indication.

Grady grinned at him. "I would have to agree," their brother Rand teased, lifting his voice above the ongoing racket. An environmentalist, he generally disliked anything that used too much energy, but for sentimental reasons made an exception when it came to Christmas lights. He lifted the boxed yard ornament from the back of his pickup truck. "I think I know who it is, too."

Although Derek was happy to see his baby brother— who was passing through Dallas on his way to a job in

East Texas—he didn't want his family nosing around in his private life. They'd already done enough of that already, questioning first his marriage and then his divorce from Carleen.

"You can't know," Derek retorted.

That was the beauty of living several hundred miles away from everyone but Grady and Alexis, who resided in nearby Fort Worth. His family couldn't usually just drop by and check in on him. It had taken big news—like the fact he was buying a home on the spur of the moment—to get his parents to drive to Dallas to see him.

Grady exchanged knowing glances with his wife and then grinned slyly. "So you admit there *is* a woman."

"No one special," Derek fibbed, growing increasingly impatient. The last thing he needed was more familial interference.

"I heard you were sweet on the Realtor who sold you this place," Rand stated. "At least that's the impression Mom and Dad got when they stopped by to congratulate you the other day."

"Mom and Dad are wrong," Derek said, noting that Alexis suddenly had a very peculiar look on her face. "Eve and I are friends. That's it." *As far as I'm going to admit at this point, anyway.*

"Good to know," a cool feminine voice said from behind him.

Swearing silently, Derek turned to confront the interloper.

Eve looked as appealing as ever, in professional garb even on a Saturday. A large embroidered carryall was slung over her shoulder, and she had a pamphlet in her hands. "This is from the neighborhood association," she said briskly. "It details their requirements for any light displays. Tells you about the parameters for taste, when they'd like the lights on and off, etcetera. I thought you would appreciate having a look at the guidelines before you got everything up."

"Thanks," Derek replied, doing his best to telegraph with his eyes that he hadn't meant what he'd just said, that he'd just been trying to keep his nosy family from interfering in their budding relationship.

If you could even call it that.

But Eve either didn't get, or didn't want to get, his message.

That impersonal look still on her face, she smiled again, gave a desultory wave and took off down the walk.

DEREK CALLED EVE several times throughout the day. She didn't pick up. Nor did she respond to any of the messages he left, asking her to phone when she had a minute.

Unwilling to let things stand with a misunderstanding of that magnitude between them, he found out where she lived and drove to her condo, a rectangular three-story building made of white stone. Luck was with him. Since it was 7:00 p.m., her car was in the lot and the lights were on in her unit.

Hoping she didn't have company over—it was Saturday night, after all—he walked up to her front door and rang the bell. Eve opened on the second ring. In a V-necked T-shirt, snug, worn jeans and shearling-lined lounging boots that came to midcalf, she looked ready for a comfortable evening at home. Her hair was tucked into a messy knot on the back of her head, and on close examination he discovered that her face was scrubbed of all makeup. Which made her skin look all the fairer. Seeing him, she sighed. "I heard you were trying to find me."

"News travels fast."

Another sigh. Her amber eyes glittering, she clamped her arms beneath her breasts. "What did you need?"

Derek noted that her delectably soft lower lip hadn't relaxed in the slightest. He dragged his gaze back to hers, swallowed around the telltale constriction in his throat. "I owe you an apology."

"No," she said sharply, "you don't."

"You misunderstood what was being said today."

She took a moment to consider that. "I think you were pretty clear, McCabe."

It was the first time she had called him by his last name. He kind of liked the reverse-intimacy of it. "I was trying to maintain my privacy."

She made a shooing motion. "So go! Maintain it!"

It was the last thing he wanted right now. Derek settled in, his shoulder braced against the door frame. "My family can be a little nosy."

She glared at him as if to say, *Beat it, buster!* Out loud, she snapped, "Not. My. Problem."

"Well, Loughlin, the fact that you're clearly mad at me is mine. And I would say it's a pretty big problem. One that needs to be dealt with right away before any more damage is done."

Scoffing, Eve folded her arms in front of her like a shield. "I would have to be interested in you to be ticked off at you."

Derek peered at her mischievously. "And you're not interested in me," he drawled, not believing it for one red-hot minute.

"Now you're getting the picture, McCabe."

There she went again with his last name. Derek

grinned. Resisting the urge to take her in his arms and kiss her until she forgot why she was so mad at him, he said instead, "Let me make it up to you."

She shrugged, demonstrating her disinterest. "There's nothing to make up."

She was wrong about that. "Have you had dinner?" Derek persisted.

Temper gleamed in her eyes and her lips clamped shut. "Again. Not your concern."

Once more Derek dug in his heels. "So you haven't," he remarked genially, as if they had just made a date, after all. "What would you like?"

A smug look on her face, she replied sweetly, "Pizza and wine. Here."

There was no "we" in that equation. *Yet.* Derek vowed to keep working on her. "Okay. Tell me exactly what you want, from which pizza place, and I'll have it delivered for you. Same with the wine."

Clearly, she was as tired of sparring with him as he was of arguing with her. Her slender shoulders began to slump. "Again, McCabe, it's really not necessary."

Derek said, even more tenderly, "Why don't you let me be the judge of that?"

She sized him up for a long, long time. Then sighed, and said finally, "You know, McCabe, just because you like to say yes a lot in your private life doesn't mean everyone else does."

This time he laughed. "Why not?" He edged closer. "It can be fun."

She didn't step back. When she finally spoke again, resignation laced her voice. "We had our fun, remember? We made love once, to satisfy our curiosity, and now we're done." She paused. "Surely some of this must sound familiar."

It did, unfortunately.

Determined to change the narrative, Derek spoke again, even more cajolingly. "Please." He held her eyes, doing what he never did—laying bare his soul. "Give me a second chance. Let me make this up to you."

EVE COULD HAVE refused a lot of things. Cool reason, a mea culpa. Teasing, or outright seduction. But to see a man like Derek practically get down on his knees and beg her to forgive him unthawed her heart. Not all the way. Just enough to allow her to open her front door and wave him in.

"You won't regret it."

She rolled her eyes, wondering what it was about this man that got to her so. "I already am."

"Has anyone ever told you that you're beautiful when you're angry?"

Eve chuckled despite herself at the dated cliché. Knowing he wasn't the kind of guy to ever deliver a line to a woman, unless it was a joke, she swatted his biceps playfully. "Watch it. Or I might put you in the deep freeze again."

He flexed his shoulders and rose to his full height. "I do not want to go there."

Eve could see that. Just as she could see how desperate he was to set things right between them. And that told her something, whether she wanted to admit it to herself or not. "What kind of pizza do you want?" she asked. If he was going to be here, they may as well eat. She was starving.

He spread his hands, obviously eager to please in whatever way necessary to get back in her good graces. "Whatever you want."

Eve groaned facetiously. "I've had a heck of a day,

McCabe. Just make a decision." Telling herself that no matter what he thought, this wasn't a date, or anything close, she handed him a take-out menu.

He glanced at it. "The Everything."

A man after her own heart. "Works for me." She let him place the order. Opened up a bottle of zinfandel and poured two glasses. "I gather Tiffany is with her mom today."

Derek clinked glasses with her. "Carleen and Craig took her to see family. They won't be back until late tomorrow evening, so I won't see her until Monday after work."

Eve settled on the sofa opposite him as they waited for their dinner. It did seem quiet without his daughter. "You must miss her."

"I do," Derek confided in a low, husky voice. "Although I'm kind of used to the schedule. And the split custody arrangement allows me time to pursue other things that are important to me."

I can't say I mind that, Eve thought. Then, realizing how premature it was for her to be thinking that way, she pushed that notion away and continued chatting casually. "I saw the yard decorations on my way home tonight." He and his family had done a great job decking out his new place. "Santa and Mrs. Claus at the North Pole. Very nice."

Derek grinned. "It was just about all the store had left, but thanks."

Their eyes met. "So how was your day?" he asked.

There was, Eve knew, only one way to describe it. "Tiring."

He listened intently, as much friend now as potential lover. "Yeah?"

Eve ran a finger down the seam of her jeans. "I finally got Flash's condo cleaned out and properly staged. We're having an open house tomorrow afternoon."

"Think it will sell now?"

"I hope so. We have only two more weeks on the listing, and he's threatening to sign with another firm if I don't get it done."

Derek's jaw flexed. Gallantly, he jumped to her rescue. "Lefleur can't blame you if he wouldn't do what was needed all this time."

"Actually, he does, and he will," Eve answered. "But enough about business." She wanted to escape from real-estate drama tonight, not wallow in it.

She stood and went to the window that looked out over the parking lot. But despite her grumbling stomach, there wasn't a delivery vehicle in sight.

Derek rose, too. "Where's your Christmas tree?" He looked past her galley kitchen, which was on the other side of the half-walled breakfast bar, and down the hall, where open doors revealed an ultrafeminine master suite, and an eight-by-ten space that seemed to be half den, half clothes closet.

Eve shrugged, suddenly feeling a little embarrassed to be living in such a small space. "I don't have one."

He turned back to her, his brow furrowed. "This year?"

She shook her head, embarrassed again. "Ever, really."

When he stepped nearer, she could see how closely he had shaved. Could smell his familiar, appealing scent. "Why not?" he asked. Eve pressed her lips together and, all too physically aware of him, paced back to the window. "Putting up holiday decorations is nothing my mother and I ever really had time to do."

Derek blinked and followed after her. "You're kidding, right?" Darkness had fallen. Although her immediate neighborhood was all brick condo units erected side by side, in the distance, colored lights twinkled and lavish homes beckoned.

She smiled. "When I was little, we had a tabletop tree—like the one I brought you and Tiffany at the hotel. But after I realized there was no Santa Claus, we stopped even that. Marjorie saw no reason for the charade."

"Christmas is a charade?"

"Expecting that miracles might happen, or that everything changes for the better this time of year, is, in my mother's view, nothing more than a fantasy, and a harmful one at that. As she's fond of saying, only hard work and clear eyes will get you where you want to go in life."

"And your perspective…?"

Of course he would ask her that. Eve sighed. "I don't know what I believe." She looked him in the eye.

"Don't know, or don't want to say?"

How about a little bit of both? Eve thought. "Not everything in life has to be definitive, Derek."

"That's true." He bent closer to study her, then murmured, "But everyone knows deep down what they believe."

Eve stiffened, unsure just how emotionally vulnerable she was ready to leave herself. "Okay," she said, with a lift of her chin. "Then tell me about you."

His blue eyes warming affectionately, he rose to the challenge. "I think Christmas is a magical time of year."

"Because…?" Eve prompted.

After pondering it for a moment, he gave her a long, telling look. "Because Christmas opens up people's hearts and makes all things seem possible."

It was certainly making *this* seem possible, she thought. She barely knew Derek, and already they felt incredibly connected. "You really are romantic, deep down," she whispered.

To her satisfaction, he didn't even try to deny it. "What does Christmas mean to you?" he asked instead.

He'd been remarkably honest. Eve knew she should be, too. Struggling to put her feelings into words, she raked her teeth across her lip. "I think it's great, if you have a big happy family, like you apparently do."

Once again, he seemed to sense all she wasn't saying. "But otherwise?" Derek tucked a strand of hair behind her ear. It was becoming a familiar gesture.

Eve savored the tender touch of his fingers against her skin. "It can be—it has been—the loneliest time of the year for me."

He smiled and dropped his hand. "Then it's time that changed."

His confidence made her laugh and groan simultaneously. "Really? And how are you going to achieve that miracle?"

"I don't know yet." He squinted, then rubbed his jaw. "But I'll come up with a plan."

Suddenly, Eve sensed they were in dangerous territory. "You're not responsible for me and my happiness."

Derek sobered, all protective male. "I know that," he told her in a low, husky voice that seemed to come straight from his heart. "But here's the thing, Eve. I want to be."

Chapter Nine

The words hung in the air between them. Derek knew it had been a cornball thing to say. It was true, nevertheless. He did want to be responsible for Eve and her happiness, in a way he'd never been with anyone before.

Problem was, she wasn't buying it. Not yet, anyway.

"Which brings me to my next question," he said. "Exactly how tired are you?"

The sparkle was back in her eyes. "Why?" she countered softly, as the doorbell rang.

Derek went to get it. He paid the pizza guy, then brought their meal back to where she was sitting, and put it on the coffee table. When he opened the box, the fragrance of fresh hot pizza filled the air.

She'd already set out stoneware plates and plenty of paper napkins. "Because," he said, returning to her side, "the evening is still young."

She glanced at the clock on the wall, noting it was half past eight. "Maybe for you. For all you know, my bedtime could be nine o'clock."

Realizing too late how that could possibly be interpreted, she flushed.

Gallantly, he let the faux pas pass, and asked instead, "What would you usually do on a Saturday night?"

A serious question deserved a serious answer. "After

a week like this past one?" Eve heaved an enormous sigh and stretched. "I'd probably bake something sweet and decadent and watch a movie."

His dark brows furrowed. "Alone?"

"Usually." Eve nodded. "I like my quiet time."

"Me, too."

For several minutes, they enjoyed their pizza in silence. Eventually, she dabbed the corners of her mouth and said, "Although, for some reason—" she winked flirtatiously "—quiet time doesn't happen a lot when you're around."

He laughed, deep and low, then waggled his eyebrows. "You never know." He left the implication hanging.

Eve looked down her nose at him like a prim schoolmarm chastising a rowdy teenage male. "I think I do."

Derek returned her slow smile with a sexy one of his own. "We could go out this evening."

She considered the possibility. "And do what?"

He smiled and took another bite of the delicious pizza.

Eve took a bite of hers, and when she'd swallowed it, said, "Obviously you have something in mind."

Derek gave a slight nod. "Something," he said, both serious and hopeful now, "that should help you get in the Christmas spirit."

"I'M NOT EXACTLY Ebenezer Scrooge," Eve drawled a few minutes later, as they cleaned up and put the leftovers in the fridge.

Derek tossed the napkins in the trash. "No one said you were."

She pushed the cork back in the wine bottle and put it away. "But you think I could use some improvement."

He folded up the pizza box. "I think your spirits could use some boosting." He reached out and rubbed the back of his hand across her cheek. "There's a difference."

Tingling from his touch, Eve went to get her jacket. Chivalrously, he assisted her as she shrugged it on. "You guarantee it's going to be worth my while."

Derek put his leather bomber jacket on. "Promise."

She grabbed her bag and together they walked out her condo door. "I don't know why I keep letting you talk me into things."

They stepped into the empty elevator and pushed the button for Lobby. "I think it's my irresistible McCabe charm," he bragged.

Eve laughed, unable to help but think how handsome he looked, no matter what time of day or night. Like the Prince Charming of her dreams. "It's something, all right," she quipped back, aware that she felt more a woman when she was with him than she had in a very long time. A woman with needs...

Oblivious to the disturbing nature of her thoughts, Derek took her hand in his. "Seriously, I promise this will make you happy."

The funny thing was, Eve realized, Derek did make her happy. Just hanging out with him on a Saturday evening made her feel giddy with excitement. And that wasn't something she'd ever experienced before.

Was this infatuation? she wondered. Or something much more?

She had no answer as Derek drove the short distance to the nearest Christmas tree lot. Set up by a local Rotary Club, it was filled with a nice selection of Fraser firs. They were about to close for the evening, but some fast talking and the promise of an extra donation from Derek kept them open a little longer.

Up and down the aisles he and Eve went. Derek looked at one after another. "What do you think?" He tucked his hand in hers and drew her close. "Seven feet tall or eight?"

Eve clasped his gloved hand and tilted her head to see his face. "Where are you going to put it?"

He looked at her as if that was an odd question. "Probably in the living room."

O-kay. Her brows came together quizzically. "You do know they're still doing construction in your home, right?"

He erupted into laughter and leaned down to touch his nose to hers. "Then it probably should go in yours."

His "Eskimo kiss" left her all aflutter. Eve drew back slightly, her eyes locked pleasurably with his. "For now," she said.

Another perplexed frown creased his handsome face. "At least until New Year's, I would think."

Eve blinked. "What are you talking about?"

Derek cupped her shoulders. "I'm buying you a Christmas tree."

She was dumbfounded.

He continued looking at her as if she wasn't the only one feeling infatuated. Persuasively, he added, "You bought me and Tiffany one, after all."

"A two-foot artificial tree." It was hardly the same thing.

"Which is perfect for us, since we're in a hotel." He went back to examining the fresh, fragrant fir he had been looking at. "This one is perfect for you."

Eve moved so he had no choice but to look at her.

She curved her hand around his biceps. "What if I don't want a tree?"

Derek curved his free hand behind his ear. "What was that you just said?" he shouted, pretending he was half-deaf. "Bah! Humbug!"

Eve laughed despite herself. She could easily see a man like this taking over her life. She could easily see *Derek* taking over her life.

He leaned down to whisper in her ear. "Come on. You know you want one."

The warmth of his breath sent a shiver down her neck. And caused new heat elsewhere.

"It's for a good cause," the Rotary volunteer interjected helpfully.

The guys had her there.

"Okay," Eve said, deciding it was less treacherous to agree than to prompt Derek to continue persuading her. "But no bigger than six feet."

"Six feet it is," Derek and the Rotarian volunteer agreed in unison.

Minutes later, they had it tied to the top of Derek's Jaguar SUV, along with a nicely decorated, fresh evergreen wreath for her door, for good measure. "Now where are we going?" she asked when they took off once again.

"Exactly where you would think." Derek parked in front of the nearest megastore with a big red-and-white circle on the front. "To buy some decorations."

They went inside together. Despite the fact it was nearly ten-thirty, the place was still packed with harried shoppers taking advantage of the extra-late holiday hours.

Derek grabbed a red plastic shopping cart, then paused to study the layout of the store. Eventually, he went left. Amazed by how at-home he was doing ordinary things, Eve trailed along after him. It seemed there were many intriguing facets to this man.

Not that he was right about everything. She tapped him on the shoulder. "If you're looking for ornaments, we should go right."

He stopped, chagrined, and smiled down at her. "I knew I brought you along for a reason."

Eve knew she had invited him in that evening for a reason. She just didn't want to think what that might be.

"So what do you think?" Derek said, as they reached the holiday decor section of the store and studied the array of possibilities.

Eve pointed out her favorites. "I like the velvet and satin bows."

He tossed several packets of each in the basket. "For the tree topper?"

It was a hard decision. "An angel," she said finally.

Derek handed her the prettiest one. "What about lights?"

Eve picked out strands of miniature colored bulbs. He put a tree stand in the cart, then moved to the next aisle. "Got to have some ornaments."

Eve bypassed everything that was breakable and went for the kid-friendly ornaments. "In case any children come over," she said with a self-conscious flush, one very special little toddler in mind.

"Safety first," Derek agreed soberly.

Eve studied their finds. "I think we've got everything."

She brought out her wallet at the checkout line. He stopped her with a shake of his head. "This is on me."

"I—"

"Consider it my thank-you to you for helping make my holidays wishes come true."

Again, they locked glances, and again something passed between them. Something tender and sweet, and undeniably uplifting.

As IT TURNED out, getting the Christmas tree into her condo was easy. Getting the trunk centered in the stand? Not so much.

First it listed to the right, then to the left. Finally, Derek got down on all fours and, lying on his side beneath the branches, adjusted it in the metal pan. While Eve held the tree in place, he tightened the bolts around the base of the trunk.

When they were both finally satisfied the tree was straight, Eve went to get water to keep it fresh. Still sprawled on the floor in a way that engendered way too many secret sexual fantasies for Eve, Derek poured in the liquid, then rose up on one elbow to hand the pitcher back.

Her pulse racing, but determined to appear unaffected, Eve set the pitcher aside and offered him a hand up. He locked palms with her, and a second later towered above her once again, all big brawny male. And Eve realized all over again this was no simple friendship. This was no simple anything.

"You okay?" he asked, peering down at her curiously.

Yes and no, Eve thought.

Somewhere in all the activity, she'd gotten her second wind. And then there was her ongoing, escalating reaction to him.

Pretending it was the holiday activity that had her

so distracted, she murmured, "Are you any good at stringing lights?"

"As it happens—" he winked at her "—I'm an ace."

He certainly seemed to know what he was doing. Curious, Eve asked, "What were your traditions like at home, when you were growing up?"

He plugged in one light strand to make sure it worked. "The usual, I guess. Stockings above the fireplace, a tree, lights inside and out, a wreath on the door."

"And socially?"

He smiled reminiscently. "It seemed like we were always busy. There were lots of extended family gatherings and community functions to attend."

It sounded…nice. Like a Hallmark movie of the way things should be. "And on the holiday itself?" she asked.

The fabric of his jeans snugly cupped his muscular thigh when he knelt to drape lights on the lower branches. "We usually had a catered dinner brought in." He threaded the strand through the fragrant evergreen and stretched it out. Their fingertips brushing, she caught it from the other side and pulled it through.

"What did you and your mom do?" he continued, equally curious.

Eve went to get another strand to plug into the first. "We went to a restaurant for dinner on Christmas Eve, opened presents on Christmas morning and usually baked cookies and watched holiday movies together later on Christmas Day." It had been really nice, and yet she'd always had the sense the holidays made her mother a little sad, so she'd been sad, too.

Derek looked at her thoughtfully. "What's your favorite movie?"

With a slightly embarrassed shrug, Eve admitted, "It's a cartoon, actually. *A Charlie Brown Christmas.*"

Derek paused. "I like that one, too. Although I never really understood Charlie Brown's melancholy until a couple years ago."

"After the whole Carleen and Craig thing…?" Eve guessed.

Derek nodded, grim. "Up until then, in a lot of ways, I'd led a charmed life."

Eve smiled up at him. "And would like to do so again."

He hunkered down to finish the lights, his sweater riding up slightly as he moved. "It'd be nice to provide Tiffany with a mommy and a daddy at both of her homes."

Dangerous territory, that. Eve tore her glance away from his flat, muscled abs. No need recalling how nice he looked naked.

Her mouth dry, she went to open up the ornaments, deliberately cutting off her view of him. "What was *your* favorite Christmas movie?"

"A Christmas Story."

Her emotions under control, Eve pivoted back to the tree and started hanging ornaments and placing velvet bows. "I don't think I've ever seen that one."

"It's set back in the late 1940s, so a lot's different than life today, but the chaos in it between siblings, and parents and children, is reminiscent of my childhood." His lip curved with amusement. "My mom used to say that her life would have been so much quieter if she'd had five girls instead of five boys."

Eve chuckled. "I wouldn't bet on that. Girls can get pretty rowdy, too. Just in different ways."

They both smiled. Then she tossed him a cookbook. He caught it one-handed. "What's this for?"

Eve stood back to admire the twinkling lights and

ornaments, and finally handed him the angel to set atop the highest branch. "You helped me with the tree. I'll bake you some cookies before I send you on your way."

He adjusted the angel, and then plugged in its cord. The angel lit up, too, adding an even more magical quality to the scene. Finished, he dusted off his hands and turned back to her, his gaze intent. "You're kicking me out?"

He didn't look as if he wanted to go any more than she wanted him to. "Eventually." She nodded at the cookbook, which he'd set aside. "What kind would you like?"

He picked it up again, an inscrutable look on his rugged face. "I can have anything I want?"

More dangerous territory—if he wanted the same thing she wanted, that was. Eve smiled and approached him lazily. "If I've got the ingredients, sure."

He flipped through the pages. "Spritz cookies."

"Chocolate or vanilla?"

"Both."

"Taskmaster," she complained.

"Hey." He angled his thumb at her chest. "You asked."

She had.

While she worked, he perused her shelves and eventually found a Chris Botti Christmas CD a client had given her. Derek slid it into the stereo and turned it on. The soothing trumpet music added a sultry aura to the apartment. Looking a bit restless and distracted himself, he returned to the kitchen and took a stool on the other side of the breakfast bar. Elbows on the counter, he watched her stuff dough into the cookie press and fit a star mold over the tip. "Is that hard to use?"

So he needed something to do with his hands, too.

With a shake of her head, Eve held it out. "Want to try?"

He rose with the same economy of motion he did everything else and strode around the counter. "I won't screw it up?"

Eve mugged comically. "If you do, we'll just reload the press with more dough and do it again."

"Well, hey, when you put it like that..."

She motioned him closer, then stepped behind him and fitted the cookie press in his big hands. "You position the end right over the baking sheet and press the trigger. That's good." She moved a bit nearer. "Keep pressing until a quarter inch or so of dough is on the sheet, then let go of the trigger and lift the press. And voilà!"

To his amazement and her delight, they ended up with a cookie shaped like a star.

"Hey, what do you know, it worked!"

Eve stepped away from him and lounged against the counter, watching. "Just keep going."

Derek pressed several more cookies in a neat row. "I am good at this."

She wrinkled her nose. "And modest, too."

He finished filling up the empty spaces on the sheet. "Helps to have a good teacher."

Eve smiled. There was no denying it—she and Derek were a good team. Wondering if there was a way for them to be friends in the future, despite the fact they'd given in to passion once already, she said, "Let's get these in the oven."

"Okay." Derek washed and dried his hands while she shut the stove door and set the timer.

He turned back to her. "Now what?"

"We do another sheet, of the chocolate ones this time."

For the next half hour, they worked side by side. Eventually, they had two more trays in and out of the oven. Delighted by their success, Eve took a warm cookie and popped it into Derek's mouth. She waited for his reaction. "Well?"

He savored the taste with the same intensity he made love. "Delicious."

She relaxed in relief. "I'm glad you like it."

"Almost," Derek added, wrapping his arms around her and tugging her close, "as delicious as you."

Eve caught her breath. "Derek…" she warned.

Eyes shuttering, he lowered his head. His lips hovered just above hers. "One kiss, Eve, before I go. That's all I'm asking."

Chapter Ten

But one kiss, Eve found, was impossible to give, never mind receive. The moment her lips fused with Derek's all common sense vanished. She arched against him, until there was only the press of hard flesh and the fierce erotic pleasure of his mouth over hers, and a kiss that seemed to go on and on and on. A kiss that was everything she had ever dreamed of…

It was the perfect Christmas gift.

But to her disappointment, it came abruptly to an end. Tensing, Derek lifted his head. He stroked his thumb across her lower lip, his eyes dark with desire. Their gazes locked, both of them breathing hard. "If you want me to leave," he warned softly, "now's the time."

She loved the brusque humor in his low tone, as much as she loved the way he looked at that moment. A little rough around the edges, and a lot aroused. "There's only one problem with that," she whispered back, lifting her hands in helpless surrender. "I don't."

One corner of his mouth crooked up. He reached for her again, dragging her against him. "Exactly what I was hoping you'd say…"

The next thing Eve knew, he had backed her against the wall. Which was good, because she was feeling a little wobbly, and the solid surface behind her helped keep her upright. Not that the hard cradle of his muscular physique wasn't doing the same. He was trapping her nicely with his big, gorgeous body and stubborn Texas resolve. He tasted innately male, like chocolate and sugar, and an essence that was unique to him. Loving every inch of him, of this, Eve pressed against him a little more. He was just as aroused, his skin burning with fiery intensity through his sweater and jeans, as he continued to kiss her, long and wet and deep.

Eventually, he lifted his head. "Here or the bed?"

Another easy decision. "Here."

He grinned and reached for her again, his blue eyes gleaming with desire and something else as well. He pushed her hair out of the way and then his lips were on the nape of her neck. "Can do."

He made her feel hot, so hot.

She held on to his shoulders with both hands as he nuzzled the sensitive place beneath her ear. His hands were moving lower, undoing the fastening of her jeans, then the zipper. The feel of his fingertips brushing against her skin made her quiver. Knees weakening all the more, she managed to gasp, "Or the bed."

He stopped what he was doing long enough to take in the sight of her. "You keep talking about Christmas presents. I think you're mine." He eased a hand past the elastic of her panties, going lower, lightly brushing back and forth. This time her knees nearly buckled, and he hadn't even found her yet.

She gasped again, still looking into his eyes. "Then that makes you mine."

His smile slow and hot, he slid a muscled thigh between her legs. "Just so you know…we're not rushing through this time."

His soft chuckle brought forth another quiver. "I'm

getting that." She leaned forward and nipped his shoulder. "It doesn't mean I'll let you have all the fun."

Throbbing all over, she eased a hand between them. Determined to give as well as receive, she worked free the buckle of his belt. He watched her with pure male satisfaction, and then he was busy, too, kissing her again, while moving his hands beneath the hem of her T-shirt, up across her ribs, to cup her breasts through the thin lace of her bra. The feel of his palms on her taut nipples sent another rush of desire through her.

"Now...inside me."

Still keeping her pinned against the wall, he lifted her so she was straddling his waist, and had no choice but to put her arms around him and hold on tight. "In time..."

His hands found her breasts; his lips found her mouth. There was nothing to do but let him have his way, and claim her he did. Without even undressing her all the way, he found a way to touch her like no one else ever had, a way that made her feel safe and wanted, pleasured and desired. Although she had promised herself she would wait for him, there was no delaying. Eve could no more control her response than she could her feelings. The next thing she knew, she was being carried down the hall to her bed. Ever so gently, he set her down. Undressed her, let her undress him.

His eyes alight with mischief and something else—something deeper than pure pleasure or want or need—he joined her.

Eve reached for him and he sprawled over her. "Are we hurrying?"

Grinning lazily, he pushed her knees apart and slid between them, settling between her spread thighs. "What do you think?"

Her hips rose to pull his body even tighter to hers. She wreathed her arms about his neck. "I think you intend to take your time."

His eyes darkening, he lowered his mouth once again. She shivered as the hardness of his chest teased the sensitive skin of her breasts into taut awareness. "Derek…" She was already so wet and so ready.

He lifted his head to look into her eyes. "Some things are worth waiting for, especially this time of year."

And wait they did, as he took her mouth again in a long, hot, tempestuous kiss. She wrapped her legs around his waist and arched up against him, enjoying the pressure of his sex nestled against hers, the intensity of his kiss, the warm cage of his arms. He kissed her until she throbbed in response, and then he kissed her some more until she clung to him and whimpered low in her throat. And only then, when they were both filled with a longing that went way beyond the physical, did he grasp her hips and slide into her, filling her completely, taking her and making her his, until she was awash in a pleasure unlike any she had ever known.

EVE WOKE HOURS later to find sunlight streaming in through the edges of the blinds. The sight of the naked man next to her was enough to make her groan.

Derek smiled and rolled onto his side. "It's a good thing we're not dating. Otherwise, who knows what would happen next, or how we would end up?"

Eve groaned again and tried, without success, to sit up. They'd made love two more times during the night and she felt as physically wrung-out as if she had run a 5k race. Wrung-out and sated. Forearm across her eyes, she stayed on her side of the bed and avoided his gaze. "It's the holidays."

Baffled, he kissed the crook of her elbow. "Meaning...?"

Grumpily, she explained, "They always leave me feeling off-kilter."

His chuckle was low and infectious. "So that's what that was."

Determined not to encourage him, Eve tamped down her own amusement. "You know what I mean." She continued to keep her face hidden, her eyes closed.

Derek rose on his elbow and gently removed her arm. "I know you keep pretending that we don't have something special, when we actually do."

Eve averted her eyes and sat up. Abruptly remembering she was naked, she clamped the top of the ice-blue satin sheet to her breasts, and then said, "Physically, yes." She couldn't exactly deny that after he'd given her innumerable orgasms through the night. And she'd given him more in return. Still smiling with masculine satisfaction, Derek lounged among the pillows. "Physically and in all the other ways that count," he corrected.

Deciding to get some clothes on before they both got turned on again, Eve disappeared into the bathroom. She came back wearing a knee-length white spa robe. "Which are?"

Looking like a Greek god who had magically landed in her bed, Derek folded his arms behind his head. "You understand me."

She didn't even understand herself! "I wish."

He stood and pulled on his shorts and then his jeans. Unfortunately for her, he looked just as mouthwatering half-clad as he had naked. He came toward her, still zipping and snapping.

"Seriously, Eve, you always know instinctively what I need. And I seem to have the same innate ability when it comes to you." He paused in front of her and continued making his case with matter-of-fact ease. "Plus, you and Tiffany get each other the same way you and I get each other. And that isn't all that common."

That was the problem—none of this was usual. She'd thought by being intensely physical when they made love, that they would be able to keep their feelings out of it. It hadn't worked; her emotions were more tangled than ever. And now Derek was doing what he did best— leaping ahead, toward his stated goal—which currently seemed to be establishing them as friends *and* lovers.

Eve released a shaky breath, more sure than ever that, at the end of all this, she was going to get hurt. "I get all that, Derek, but this is still happening way too fast."

He looked at her, his eyes warm and assessing, even as she struggled to get a handle on herself. "Or not fast enough," he drawled.

She was saved from having to reply by the ringing of her phone.

She went to get it. "Obviously, you haven't been checking your messages," Marjorie said.

Eve knew that tone. She sat down on the edge of the bed, filled with dread, while Derek lingered nearby, watching her with concern. "What happened?"

"Sibley & Smith brokered another sale last night, which puts them ahead of us in the sales race."

Eve signaled to Derek that he didn't have to worry about the call. He nodded and slipped out of the room to give her privacy.

With him gone, Eve was able to concentrate on the problem at hand. "By how much?" she asked her mother.

"Close to one and a half million."

Eve rubbed her suddenly aching forehead. "You're sure?"

Marjorie scoffed. "I wouldn't be calling you if I wasn't."

"There's still time for us to move ahead again, Mom. Flash's condo was finally staged the way it should have been all along. We're having an open house there this afternoon."

Her mother sighed, her pessimism apparent. "Even if it sells today it won't be enough."

"Astrid and Vanessa are pushing their own properties hard, too," Eve added, comforting her mother the best she could.

Marjorie's voice was suddenly tearful. "I thought we finally had it this year." So had Eve. This was exactly the kind of tension and stress none of them needed, particularly now.

Worried about more important matters than just the sales race, she asked, "How's your heart?"

"Broken!" her mother cried. "What do you think?"

Well, at least she wasn't being overly dramatic. "I meant medically, Mom. You're not having any chest pains again, are you?"

There was another pause. "No. I'm not. My heart is fine, honey." Her mother spoke again, contrite this time. "I'm sorry if I upset you."

This was new. Marjorie never apologized for venting or anything else. Eve walked out into the living room. Derek was fully dressed and making coffee, giving her a glimpse of what it would be like to have him around all the time. Very nice.

With effort, she focused on the situation at hand. "Are you sure you are okay, Mom?"

"I'm fine."

Eve relaxed in relief. "I'll see you this evening, then, for dinner, after the open house."

They said goodbye and hung up.

"Everything okay?" Derek asked.

This would be a good place to draw a line. To tell him thanks but no thanks. Unfortunately, Eve knew she needed to confide in someone. And right now that someone was Derek.

She went into the kitchen and brought out two mugs, as well as some pastries from the bakery. "My mother is fine, although how long she will stay that way if Vanessa, Astrid or I don't make another big sale is anyone's guess." While Derek listened intently, she explained about the annual Highland Park home-sales race.

He poured coffee for both of them. "Sounds like a pretty big deal."

Eve added creamer to hers. "It is. My mother has come close before, but she's never won it, so to have the lead in the competition for most of the latter part of this year, only to lose it right after her heart attack, is devastating for her."

Derek guided Eve to a stool at the breakfast bar and sat down next to her. "Should you go and see her?"

Eve picked at her cranberry-and-almond scone. "Right now? Heavens, no! The only thing my mother wants me doing at the moment is working on making another sale."

Derek broke a blueberry scone in two. "I'm assuming you have other leads."

"I do. I just need to pursue them more aggressively." *And stop putting so much time and attention into my personal life. At least for now...*

"YOU'RE LOOKING GOOD," Eve told her mother in surprise, hours later. Sunday evening, the rehab center cafeteria was sparsely populated with patients and families, but her mom had saved a table for the two of them in a far corner.

Her cheeks pink with excitement, Marjorie smiled. "I feel better. The yoga workouts they have me doing are really helping me deal with stress."

Eve set out the glasses of decaf iced tea and grilled chicken entrée plates she had picked up in the line, then moved the plastic tray aside. "That's good to hear." Although she still worried that her mother would be able to pace herself as directed, when she was finally permitted to return to work.

Marjorie took two small bites, then pulled a small leather-bound notepad and a pen out of her pocket. "As long as I have you here, I have a few reminders."

Eve paused, her fork halfway to her mouth. "Are the doctors okay with you doing this?"

"Within reason, yes." Marjorie put on her diamond-studded reading glasses and flipped to the correct page. "First of all, don't forget the annual black-tie Highland Park Holiday Gala on the seventeenth of December." The proceeds of which went to a host of local charities.

Because it was something she and her mother typically did together, Eve murmured, "I was thinking I might skip it this year."

Marjorie straightened in alarm. "Don't you dare! It's more important than ever, in the wake of my heart attack, that Loughlin Realty be well represented. I've already given my ticket away, but I presume you still have yours?"

Eve swallowed a bite of steamed broccoli. She'd also made a considerable donation on behalf of the firm. "Yes."

"Good. Then I expect you to go. Next, I know you're

discouraged about the sales race. Astrid and Vanessa were, too, when I spoke with them. But there's no need to be, because I just got off the phone with Red Bloom."

Doing her best to keep her manner neutral, Eve asked mildly, "Red Bloom called you?"

"Actually, I phoned him. I asked him to reconsider the Santiago Florres house."

Eve tensed. Her mother sometimes had the tendency to push too hard. When she did, the results were often not positive. "And?"

"He remains fascinated by the architecture, and turned off by the asking price."

Eve frowned, frustrated, because her mother could have inadvertently put a kink in the solution Eve was working on behind the scenes. She sat up straight. "I thought you wanted me to handle this, Mom."

Marjorie gave her a look of innocence. "I do."

Eve tried not to be hurt by her lack of faith. "Then trust me to do so, Mom." She sighed wearily. "And in the meantime, there's something *you* can do for *me*. Concentrate on getting better so I won't have to spend so much time worrying about you."

Her mother looked slightly taken aback by Eve's entreaty. Silence fell and the two women resumed their meals. After a few long, tense minutes, Marjorie finally set her fork down and turned to her daughter. "You can sell the Santiago Florres home to Red Bloom with the right approach, Eve. And if you do…"

"We'll win the sales race." Eve guessed where all this was going.

"But just in case neither of those options work out, there is one other alternative," Marjorie continued stubbornly. "I know you've been spending a lot of time with Derek McCabe."

Probably too much, Eve thought, given how huge a part Derek and his daughter had started to play in her life in such a short amount of time.

"I also know that when he came to us, he originally intended to invest seven to eight million dollars in real estate before the end of the year. I imagine some of that cash is going into the fixer-upper he bought."

"A fair amount, actually," Eve conceded.

"But that still leaves a lot of money to invest somewhere else."

Her mother did not need to tell her there was more money to be made here. Normally, this was an opportunity Eve would be pursuing with all her might. Her growing feelings for Derek, however, made even the idea of taking things back to a strictly business level both unpalatable and upsetting. Although she might not know exactly what they were feeling besides lust and longing, and an increasingly intimate friendship, she was sure she didn't want whatever this was with him to end. And certainly not for business reasons.

Impatiently, Eve asked, "What exactly are you suggesting, Mom?"

"That you leverage your friendship with him, and use your powers of persuasion to help Derek meet his original investment goals. And in the process, help make Loughlin Realty the winner in this year's Highland Park sales race."

Winning top honors appealed to Eve, although clearly not as much as it did to her mother. Using Derek did not.

"Of course, I could call him and broach the topic, if you'd prefer," Marjorie offered. "Perhaps suggest he use Vanessa or Astrid as the agent, if you're not able to help."

Eve ignored the unspoken question: What exactly was stopping her from jumping on this opportunity?

"Thanks," she said, stifling a beleaguered sigh. She knew the last thing Derek probably wanted or needed was a hard sell from her mother, or the other agents in the office. "But—" *if it must be done, and I wish to heck it didn't* "—I'll do it."

Chapter Eleven

Eve was already waiting when Derek walked into the hotel bar. She had a glass of sparkling water with lime in front of her, a frown pursing her soft lips.

Derek slid into the cozy leather booth opposite her. Like her, he'd spent the day working. Now, at 8:00 p.m., he was ready for a little rest and relaxation.

"I'm glad you called." Although he couldn't say he was totally surprised, given what he had received via messenger that afternoon. "It was my second surprise of the day."

Their eyes locked and he felt the connection between them deepen.

"What was the first?"

The mystified note in her voice made him smile. "The ticket from your mother."

Eve blinked, then stared at him in confusion.

Derek leaned closer, inhaling a whiff of her hyacinth perfume. On impulse, he covered her hand with his. "For the Highland Park Holiday Gala on the seventeenth?"

The breath stalled in her throat, while her cheeks flushed with color. "Mom sent you that?"

"Along with the suggestion that I might attend with you, if I didn't want to go alone."

Eve inhaled sharply. He tightened his grip on her hand, feeling the omnipresent need to protect her. "I take it that it wasn't your idea?"

Eve glanced away, clearly struggling to remain impassive. "No. I didn't know anything about it until just now."

Disappointment moved through him. "You don't have to go with me," he pointed out gruffly, releasing her hand and sitting back.

She lifted her chin, for a second putting decorum and expectation aside. The way she looked at him let him know her pride was on the line. "And vice versa."

He couldn't blame her for being upset; he wouldn't want his family setting up social engagements for him, either. On the other hand, this was a prime opportunity for them to be together in another not-really-a-date-even-if-it-feels-like-a-date way.

He let his gaze drift over her, taking in the snug fit of her clothes and the heart on a chain nestled in the V of her black cashmere sweater. Appreciating the fact she'd done something different with her hair again— tonight it was styled in sophisticated waves that tumbled to her shoulders—he grinned at her as if this was no big deal, after all.

"However, I wouldn't mind going to a black tie event with you on my arm." Then he winked at her for good measure, in case she needed more encouragement to override her pride. "Especially since the gala benefits all the Highland Park charities, and it would be a great opportunity for you to introduce me around to all the movers and shakers in this town."

Eve paused and wet her lips. Finally, she admitted, "I wouldn't mind attending with you, either."

Derek had an idea what it had cost her to say yes,

especially to such a public function that might cause one heck of a lot of gossip and speculation about their relationship.

To lighten the mood, he teased, "So is it a… I was going to say date, but—" he pulled out his phone and pretended to look at his calendar "—we're not scheduled to have that until January 15 of next year, so…"

This time Eve grinned, and soon after, a soft laugh escaped her.

Derek chuckled, too, finally feeling as if they were on the right track again. He signaled the bartender and asked for a draft beer and an order of Southwestern egg rolls.

She sipped her sparkling water. He shifted a little, trying to get comfortable in the cozy space. In the process, his knees briefly brushed hers beneath the table. Like him, she was wearing slacks and soft leather boots. Unlike him, she seemed to have a lot on her mind that was still troubling her.

"So what's happening?" he asked. Why had she requested to meet him in the bar instead of his hotel suite? Why did she still seem so reserved?

Abruptly, her manner turned professional. "I wanted to talk business with you."

That was a little bit of a letdown, Derek acknowledged privately. But then again, any reason to spend time with her was appreciated. Telling himself he should accept the time with her for the gift it was, he accepted his beer and sipped the mellow brew. "Fire away."

The waiter returned with a platter of piping-hot appetizers, garnished with pico de gallo, guacamole and sour cream. Derek took one of the serving plates and handed it to her. He kept the other for himself.

Eve helped herself to an egg roll. "You said you were

still interested in investing in property before the end of the calendar year."

That, Derek thought, was even more of a disappointment. He cut through the crispy golden-brown skin, revealing a mixture of gooey melted cheese, spicy peppers, black beans and diced white chicken. "That's right. I am."

Eve carefully spread her napkin across her lap. "I'd like to help you with that."

He added condiments to his plate. "You don't think it will make things too complicated?"

Eve sliced into her egg roll, too. "We could put whatever this is on hold until after any transaction is complete."

Derek didn't want to spend the holidays pretending he wasn't interested in her. Aware this was where he drew the line, he speared her with a brutally honest glance, and then murmured, "What if I don't want to put whatever this is between us on hold? What if I want to do both simultaneously?"

Eve swallowed with difficulty. She continued holding his gaze and said, "Here's the thing. I don't want to be seen as unfairly influencing you."

Derek waved off the possibility. "No one who knows me would ever think that could happen."

Eve went back to eating. "So you'd be okay with this?" she asked casually.

"Absolutely." He paused to study her evasive expression. "Although, I have the feeling that this wasn't your choice in the matter." That she wouldn't even be suggesting it, if not for the pressure at the firm to meet year-end sales goals in wake of her mother's unexpected absence.

Eve straightened. She flashed another businesslike

smile. "I admit I prefer to work in a more leisurely fashion." She took another dainty bite. "I also know, for a variety of reasons, that it isn't always possible. So I'm prepared to adapt."

"So am I," Derek said, glad she was finally meeting him halfway.

Eve visibly relaxed. "When would you like to get started?"

Damned if she wasn't the most beautiful woman he had ever known, no matter what kind of light she was in, Derek mused to himself. And damned if he didn't want her in the worst way. Sensing that would never change, he forced himself to get back on track.

"Tiffany and I are headed to my hometown of Laramie, Texas, the weekend before Christmas."

Eve quickly brought up the calendar on her phone. "The nineteenth?"

"Yes. So if you'd like to accompany me, and see the ranch I've got my eye on, then that would be great."

Eve finished typing and set her phone down. "You want to buy property in Laramie County?"

Derek nodded. "There's a ranch there that's not on the market yet, but it will be after the New Year. I'd like you to see it. Maybe help me negotiate a deal on the property before it's even listed." Derek could tell by the look on her face that she wasn't surprised by his aggressive tactics. She knew that was how he operated when it came to business, that only the first-on-the-scene got results.

"So long as you know that area is not my premier stomping ground," Eve cautioned.

Derek took another sip of beer. "I'm confident you have the tools to assess proper market value."

"Okay, then, that's great. I'm looking forward to it."

She made a note on the calendar on her phone, then glanced up, with the same stressed-out expression in her eyes he had seen when he'd first walked in.

Derek caught her wrist before she could attempt to leave. "So now that that's set," he said huskily, wanting to help her the way she always helped him, "do you want to tell me what's really bothering you?"

ONCE AGAIN, Eve thought, Derek had read her like a book.

"Did the open house at Flash's condo not go well?"

Eve shrugged. "It went fine."

"Then...?"

His eyes fell on her, full of warmth and tenderness. "You don't want to hear this," she said irritably.

"Yes. I do."

Knowing she had to unburden herself to someone, and that, irrationally, she wanted that someone to be Derek, she briefly explained the way her mother had undermined her with a Houston-based client.

"Is she this way with everyone, or just you?"

Eve gestured helplessly, even as she appreciated Derek's support. "Pretty much everyone."

He looked at her with compassion. "But it still hurts." He took her hand again, and this time didn't let go. "You wish she had more faith you."

Eve basked in the protectiveness of his grasp. "I do."

Derek's gaze roved her face. "Have you told your mom that?"

She stifled a groan. "Oh, yes."

He flashed a sympathetic half smile. "And Marjorie's response...?"

Eve grimaced. "To tell me how to do whatever it is I'm trying to do, only better."

Derek let out a low chuckle. "Sounds like a parent."

Eve pouted. "It's not funny."

His glance turned tender once again. "I know, but what are you going to do?" He shrugged in a way that encouraged her to let it go and move on. "Especially when you know you're going to get that Santiago Florres house sold."

Eve didn't protest when he took her other hand, too. "How can you be so sure?"

"You're telling me you don't have a plan to accomplish your goal?" He held her hands gently.

"Well, I do have a little something I've been working on...."

"See?" he said bracingly. "It's all going to work out in the end."

"Thank you for boosting my spirits tonight."

"Now," Derek said, "how about you do a little something to help me?"

EVE HAD COME here tonight hoping to get things back on a purely business track with Derek. Instead, she had ended up pouring her heart out to him and feeling even that much closer.

The unexpected outcome should have worried her. Encouraged her to take yet another step back from the prospect of falling so hard for him that she would never be able to recover, if and when this whatever-it-is they were sharing came to an end.

But sitting with him in the dimly lit hotel bar, with Christmas music playing softly in the background, all she could think was that spending all this time with him was making this the best holiday season she had enjoyed in years. *If ever.*

Before she could stop herself, she leaned toward him and murmured, "What did you need?"

Derek grimaced.

It was, Eve thought, his turn to look uncertain and disgruntled.

"I think I should get Tiffany a baby doll for Christmas. The problem is, I can't figure out which one to get."

Eve smiled, as ready to help him as he had been to assist her. "Did you have any particular type of doll in mind?"

He sighed. "I went over to the doll store in the Galleria Mall this afternoon."

Eve approved. "That is the place to go."

"Yeah, well, I was pretty overwhelmed." He shook his head. "As I soon as I walked in, I realized I was way out of my league."

"Isn't there someone you could ask?"

He made a comical face. "I am."

It had been a long time since Eve was a kid. "I'm not an expert."

Affection lit his eyes. "You know my little girl, though. And unless I miss my guess, you probably had dolls when you were growing up."

Another wrong perception. Reluctantly, Eve admitted, "Actually, my mom favored educational toys. Or in other words, she didn't want me spending all my time playing house when I could be learning about the ins and outs of real estate."

Derek stared at her as if he didn't know what to make of that. "You're kidding."

Eve sighed and rested her chin in her hands. "I wish."

He caught the check before she could get it. "So you really don't know anything about dolls?"

In frustration, Eve watched the waiter walk off with Derek's bank card instead of hers. "I know Tiffany will like anything that you get her. Especially a baby doll."

Derek threw up his hands. "Which leads us back to square one. How do I pick out the right one for her?"

Silly man. "Why don't you let her do that?"

He lifted a brow.

"Take Tiffany to the big doll store at the Galleria and let her *show* you which one she likes," Eve suggested practically.

Derek stroked his jaw, clearly liking the idea. "I hadn't thought of that." Then he turned to her. "I have one more question." Eve waited with bated breath, certain without him even saying it that this involved her somehow.

"Will you go with us?"

She knew if she had one ounce of common sense left, one flicker of hope for keeping her expectations from going way out of bounds—and her heart from being broken—she should say no. "Sure," she heard herself saying instead.

Derek accepted his bank card and receipt. They rose.

"Six o'clock tomorrow night okay with you?" he asked, walking her out to the front of the hotel, where they waited for the valet to bring her car.

"Sounds good," Eve returned, even as she continued to wonder what she was doing, getting in so far, so fast. It had to be the season.

"Great." Derek leaned down and gently touched his lips to hers. "Tiffany and I will see you then."

"DOLL SHOPPING, HMM?" Sasha said the following day.

Eve flushed, beginning to regret asking the three moms of daughters in their office for their advice on which of the exclusive dolls would be best to buy for a one-year-old. She wanted to be able to steer Derek to the right area in the store, in case Tiffany had limited patience for looking. "Don't razz me."

Astrid lifted both her hands. "We wouldn't think of it."

Vanessa's brow furrowed. "Are the two of you dating?"

"No," Eve said.

At the same moment Derek walked into the office and said, "Yes." At her scathing glare, he added, "Unofficially."

Sasha, Astrid and Vanessa all smiled. Which was no surprise. All three of them were happily married and, unlike her mother, had been urging Eve for some time to perk up her social life.

Eve shut off her computer and slid her tablet and phone into her bag. Desperate to get the conversation on more neutral ground, she asked cheerfully, "Where's Tiffany?"

Derek lounged in the doorway. "Still waiting for us to pick her up."

Eve sent her coworkers a look that said, *See? We're going to be well chaperoned by a demanding one-year-old. It's not what you think, after all.*

They didn't buy it.

Unable to bear the scrutiny, Eve slipped out the door.

"So how was your day?" Derek asked. His arm slid around her waist as he walked her to his SUV.

Tingling, she eased away and climbed into the passenger seat. "Good. One of the Realtors who was at the open house at Flash's condo called today to find out how far below the asking price he might be willing to go." Modestly, she tucked her skirt around her legs.

Derek slipped behind the wheel. "Think you're going to get a bid?"

"My guess is, if all goes the way we like, by the end of the week."

Pleasure lit his handsome features. "That is good."

Eve nodded in agreement.

"Any luck with the Santiago Florres house?"

"I talked to both parties to see if I could get them to meet in the middle."

"And?"

"No go. So now I'm tracking down Florres himself. I'm hoping he'll be interested in meeting the investor and to talk about the house he designed and built, explain why the property is so unique, and hence, worth the asking price."

"Hmm. Nice approach."

"Thank you." Eve grew pensive. "I just hope it works."

Fortunately, all talk of business soon faded.

Tiffany was happy to see Derek after a weekend away, and just as happy to see Eve. She babbled all the way to the mall, and was still grinning when they entered the Galleria. She was too excited to sit in the stroller, so Eve pushed the empty carriage alongside Derek while he carried his little girl in his arms.

Tiffany was even more delighted when they entered the beautifully appointed doll store. It was filled with little girls of all ages and their parents, all gazing raptly at the amazing array of dolls and accessories. Eve wasn't surprised to see a number of shoppers from the Highland Park area, people she had met or knew casually from her years in the real estate business. More than once, she found herself waving or mouthing hello as she directed Derek to the section that held the My First Baby Doll designs.

"I think I know which one she likes," he said eventually.

A doll with light skin, red hair and blue-gray eyes.

Eve had seen Tiffany go back to that one again and again. "You want to find a clerk?" The models that were out were only for display.

Derek nodded. He handed Tiffany over to Eve. "I'll be right back."

Eve snuggled Tiffany close, the now-familiar weight in her arms feeling as good as her sweet baby smell. Tiffany enjoyed the cuddling, too. "Mommy," she said, patting Eve's cheeks.

Eve was about to correct her, when behind her, she heard a strident feminine voice. "Well, as I live and breathe. Eve Loughlin, I knew you'd succumb to the joys of motherhood, just like the rest of us!"

Eve turned to see a former college classmate. Linda Brashear had been the president of the women's business club until she'd left school to get married. She was one to never let anything—or anyone—go without putting in her two cents.

Eve forced a smile. "Linda, hi." The two women hugged, Texas-style. "It's been forever," she said.

Linda beamed. "Hasn't it?"

"Mommy," Tiffany repeated even more joyously, once again patting Eve's cheeks.

"I didn't know you got married," Linda continued, her eyes widening in surprise.

"I, um, haven't," Eve said uncomfortably, just as Derek rejoined them.

"Daddy!" Tiffany said, arms outstretched for him.

"Well," Linda said, still seeming a little shocked as

she looked Derek's big, strapping form up and down, "I can see why you'd be willing to forgo the legalities. Although," she sniffed, "now that you two have a little one, I would think—"

"We probably should get married," Derek interjected. Sensing correctly that she was ripe for rescue, he wrapped his arm around Eve's shoulders and tugged her close to his side.

Linda, who had never been shy about voicing an opinion on anyone's love life, heartily agreed with him. "You-all really should. Although—" she elbowed Derek playfully "—I have to congratulate you for getting her this far. Because Eve always said she was never ever going to have kids."

"WANT TO TALK about it?" Derek asked quietly half an hour later. Clearly, Eve thought, he felt they should.

Their purchase completed, they were sitting in the doll store bistro housed on the upper floor of the enormous space. Specially designed for little girls, the elegant restaurant sported white linen tablecloths and dinnerware that was ultrafeminine and still child-friendly.

Happy to be away from the crowds and chaos below, Eve busied herself cutting up the mini pretzel balls from the appetizer plate for Tiffany to munch on. She slid them over onto the toddler's high-chair tray.

If only they hadn't run into Linda Brashear! Ever since Eve had known the other woman, she'd had a reputation for being a real busybody.

Not that Eve could keep something like this from Derek forever.

Still feeling a little chagrined by her former friend's

disclosure, Eve forced herself to lift her chin and meet his eyes. "What do you want to know?"

Seemingly as on edge as she felt, Derek helped himself to a baby carrot. Eventually, he asked, "Is it true? Did you vow never to have kids?"

Eve wanted to lie, even though she knew she couldn't. "Yes. I did." She took a strawberry-and-cheese kabob for herself.

He sent her another guarded look. "Why didn't you want children?"

Tiffany lounged back in her seat and contentedly watched the other diners. Aware how much of a family they felt at times like this, how much she had grown to love it, Eve swallowed. Would Derek think less of her if she told him everything? Finally, she said, "It's complicated."

His blue eyes glimmered with interest. "I've got time."

Of course he did. He always did. Aware they were about to enter an emotional minefield, she chose her words carefully. "I guess I've never really seen myself as being lucky enough to find a guy who would love me forever. It doesn't really run in the family, you know? And I didn't want to go the route my mother went and be a single mom." Eve took a sip of peppermint tea, then shook her head. "It was just too hard."

Derek studied her with the kindness she had come to rely on. "For her or for you?" he asked.

She flashed a rueful smile. "For both of us. My mom was always working. I always wanted more of her time. It seemed like neither of us ever got what we wanted and needed from each other when I was growing up. And—" her voice caught "—I didn't want to put a child through that."

Too late, she realized the implication of what she'd said. Derek himself was a single parent—at least half the time, anyway. Eve stared at him in chagrin. "I'm sorry. I shouldn't be talking like this."

His eyes darkened with a mixture of compassion and sorrow. He leaned toward her and captured her hand. "Why not?"

"Because..." She looked down at their intertwined fingers, taking comfort in both his strength and his refusal to let her drift away, as she was otherwise likely to do. "I don't want you to think that your situation will be as tough as mine was, because our situations aren't the same." Wary of stepping in where she didn't belong, Eve treaded carefully. "You have Carleen, and Craig and their kids, and your extended families. Tiffany is going to have plenty of people in her life who will be there for her. She's never going to feel like a burden."

There was no judgment in his eyes, only curiosity. "Is that the way you felt? Like a burden?"

Eve released the breath she'd been holding. How was it Derek could see what no one else did? Reluctantly, she conceded, "Sometimes, but that's as much my fault as hers. I know my mom did the best she could under what were very tough circumstances. She gave me a good life and I owe her a lot."

Derek's hand tightened on hers. He seemed to understand that she loved her mom very much, and always had. "Do you still not want to have kids?"

Eve was beginning to want it all. And that scared her more than she wanted to admit. "If I was married, then yes, I would definitely want children."

He paused. "But not as a single parent."

She conceded with a nod, withdrew her hand from

his and said emphatically, "For me, it would be just too hard."

Again, he understood. His lips crooked ruefully. "Having done it on my own, even half the time, for the past year, I agree." His deep blue eyes met hers. "It is hard raising a child on your own."

Aware, as always, that Derek had options most people did not, Eve suggested, "You could always get a nanny for backup."

He shook his head. "That's not the same as having a mommy and a daddy in residence."

Eve had certainly missed having both. "True," she said with a sigh.

She looked at him, and realized this was striking a chord with him. She thought back to that conversation when he'd confided his desire that Tiffany have equal love and happiness in both households where she lived.

"Which is why," Derek continued, even more firmly, "one day soon I intend to get married again."

Chapter Twelve

Eve stared at Derek in shock. Once again, he knew he had pushed her too hard, too fast.

"You can't just decide that without having anyone in mind," she declared, aghast.

Who says I don't have anyone in mind? Derek thought to himself. But aware it was far too soon to be hammering Eve with that, he shrugged. "Getting married again in the very near future is still one of my goals." She looked so indignant, he couldn't help but tease, "Like not getting too involved is one of yours."

Her lips curved ruefully as his joke hit home. "You're cute."

"Thank you." Derek preened comically, while Tiffany giggled and waved her baby spoon at both of them. "I'm constantly being told so."

Eve rolled her eyes.

Derek smiled, although he wished she had said that, like him, she was looking forward to tying the knot sooner rather than later.

The waiter appeared with their entrées: macaroni and cheese for Tiffany, quiche Florentine and salad for Eve, a chicken pot pie for Derek.

Derek sobered. He wanted to nail down their next

non-date, or two or three. "So what are your plans for tomorrow?" he asked.

Eve mugged at Tiffany, who mugged back. Then, still grinning, she pulled out her phone and checked her calendar. "I've got appointments all day."

"Clients?"

She nodded and continued scrolling through the day. "A quick dinner with my mom at cardiac rehab, then shopping tomorrow evening."

He widened his eyes, intrigued.

She grinned at his continued teasing, and explained, "I have to get a dress for the gala."

"Hmm. I could help with that."

Amusement lit her eyes, along with a hint of desire. "I bet you could, Mr. McCabe. But no. Thanks, anyway."

She just wouldn't let them get close, Derek thought ruefully. "That's okay. I like to be surprised." Letting her know with a glance that he wasn't about to give up on either her or them, he flashed a smile. "So what time am I picking you up on the seventeenth?"

Eve fed Tiffany a little more of her macaroni and cheese so Derek could concentrate on his own entrée. "Seven-thirty okay with you?"

He nodded, ready to be as patient as he needed to be. "Seven-thirty is great." *Any time I'm with you is great.*

As comfortable as if she really was the "mom" in this equation, Eve turned back to him amenably. "How's your house renovation coming, by the way?"

Derek imagined her living in the house with him. Making love every night, waking up in the morning wrapped in each other's arms. "I'm set to move in on December 18."

"Really?"

He nodded in anticipation. "Want to come over and celebrate our first night in the new home with Tiffany and me?"

Excitement sparkled in Eve's amber eyes. Still, it took her a moment to say yes. "What should I bring?"

The only thing he really wanted and needed, Derek thought. He smiled again. "Just yourself."

"HOW SERIOUS ARE you about Derek McCabe?" Sasha asked Eve several days later.

Eve walked out of the conference room, where she had just signed another post-holiday home listing. "Why?"

"He called this morning and was fishing for information on what kind of gift you might like for Christmas."

"Tell me you're kidding."

"I am not kidding."

"Was it— Was he—?"

Sasha grinned. "Use your words."

Eve tried again. "Are we in the category of a thank-you-for-helping-me-buy-a-house gift?"

"I don't know. Does jewelry fall into that?"

She sucked in a breath. "I don't suppose we're talking costume jewelry."

"Hmm." Sasha struck a thoughtful pose. "The man makes millions." She considered some more, then straightened. "I kind of don't think so."

Eve flushed in embarrassment. "Well, I can't accept anything extravagant!" It would mean... Well, she wasn't sure what it meant, but nothing casual, of that she was certain. Derek did not do casual, in his work or personal life. He was either all in or all out.

The office manager tilted her head. "Calm down."

She patted Eve on the back. "He hasn't given anything to you yet."

Sasha was right. Eve knew she was overreacting. Determined not to be so transparent with her emotions, she drew a deep breath and went back to her desk, where yet another stack of messages awaited her. Knowing how busy he was, she imagined it was the same for Derek. "Did he say anything else?"

The other woman grinned and handed her a few more papers, all relating to another listing about to close. "Besides wanting to know what your birthstone was, you mean?"

Birthstone? That sounded better. Eve breathed a sigh of relief. "You told him garnet?"

"Duh." Sasha smiled as she adjusted the blinds on the window. "He wanted to know what kind of diamond you prefer, too."

Was it hot in here or what? Eve fanned herself with the stack of papers in her hand. "Holy…"

"Moly, I know."

She had heard of women being romanced this way. Many of her well-heeled clients had been. But it had never happened to her. Eve tugged the neckline of her silk blouse away from her collarbone. "Maybe he's just…"

Sasha peered at her, sensing as accurately as Marjorie had that something was up between Derek and Eve. Or had been on several occasions now. "What?"

"I don't know." Eve brushed a hand through her hair and sank down in her chair. Just thinking about Derek in that capacity made her heart race and her knees go weak.

Sasha lingered a moment longer. 'What are you getting him?"

Eve fanned herself again. "Um, some sort of house-warming gift for the get-together, when he moves into his house." A get-together that as far as she knew included only three people: Derek, Eve and Tiffany. How family-oriented was that?

Sasha walked back to the break room and returned with two bottles of water. She handed one to Eve. "You're getting him a plant?"

Eve uncapped the bottle and took a long drink of the ice-cold water. She waved an airy hand, glad she didn't have to meet with a client right this minute and instead could take the time to compose herself. "He doesn't really seem like the watering can kind of guy."

Sasha quirked her lips and perched on the window-sill. "I didn't think so, either."

Feeling even more uncomfortable, Eve rocked back in her desk chair, muttering under her breath, "This is the part of Christmas I hate." Deciding there was something wrong with the ergonomic adjustments, she reached under the seat to alter the forward tilt. To no avail. It still seemed…off-kilter, somehow.

Sasha watched as she stood up and looked under the chair. "So you *are* dating?"

Frustrated, Eve got down on her knees. "I don't know what we're doing." That was the problem. But now she had to get him a gift. At least for the housewarming. And probably Christmas as well, unless she wanted to look like the kind of person who took and never gave back.

But what? What could she get him? Should she get Tiffany something, too?

Just because she and Derek had made love a few times—and he intended to get married again someday soon—did not make them an item. They weren't even

dating yet. It was all too complicated. Way too complicated. Although buying a present for Tiffany would be
easy. All Eve would have to do was go to the doll store
at the Galleria Mall and pick out an accessory for her
new baby doll. Derek was another matter.

Eve attempted another adjustment, then sat down
once again. The tilt was worse than before.

She swore, frustrated beyond measure.

Once again, Sasha walked out and sauntered back
in. "Cheer up." She tossed a stack of holiday sale cata-
logues on Eve's desk. "McCabe's probably got everything there is to have, so anything you get will be a
duplicate, anyway."

Eve groaned loudly and massaged her temples.
"Thank you for pointing that out. And for the record,
if he wasn't still a client…"

"You'd already be hooked up with him?"

Guilt roared through her like a tidal wave.

Sasha gasped in shock. "*Have* you hooked up?"

Wishing she had a better poker face—when it came
to Derek and her feelings about him, anyway—Eve
lifted a hand and waved off any further questions.

Sasha's grin widened. Eve noted that her friend
hadn't looked that happy and optimistic since she had
fallen in love with the man of her own dreams and
headed off down the aisle.

It was Christmas, that was all, a season that had so
much romance in the air.

Belatedly, Eve realized she should have kept to her
usual "Bah, Humbug" script.

After another considering look, Sasha quipped, "Did
anyone ever tell you that you're cute when you're falling in love?"

This time Eve blushed fire-engine red. It was hot

as blazes in here. "I am not." She got up to check the thermostat. Seventy degrees! It could not possibly be seventy. It felt like ninety!

"You are falling in love," Sasha insisted with a knowing wink. "You just can't admit it yet. But have faith. In time, you will." The happily married Sasha sauntered out, calling over her shoulder, "And good luck with your dress shopping tonight!"

The door shut behind her.

Eve groaned loudly and dropped her head down on her desk. The only good thing was that she wasn't seeing Derek for several more days. She needed time apart—make that a lot of time apart—so she could come to her senses and keep from falling into bed with him yet again.

TIME APART WAS not the least bit helpful, Eve decided the evening of December 17, when Derek showed up at seven twenty-five.

Incredibly good-looking under normal circumstances, he was devastatingly handsome in black tie. He smelled heavenly, too. Like sandalwood and birch and cardamom.

She, on the other hand, was not at all ready. Her hair and makeup were done, but her dress was only half-zipped, and she couldn't find one of her shoes. Or any of the jewelry she wanted to wear. Although why that was, she hadn't a clue.

"Take it easy. We've got time." He gestured for her to turn around. His hands brushed her bare skin as he tugged the zipper up. Finished, he paused to kiss the nape of her neck. "I like the dress." He caught her hand and spun her around, eyeing her sparkly cranberry-red strapless gown appreciatively. Blatant desire tugged at the corners of his mouth. "You look good in red."

Eve knew she might as well be honest. She paused to straighten his bow tie, then stepped back to make sure it was centered. Her glance caught his. "You look good, too." Almost too good. Standing here with him, she was tempted to never even make it to the event.

Derek smiled. "Perhaps we should join a mutual admiration society."

Noting he hadn't brought any jewelry with him, Eve laughed and began to relax. "Why don't you make yourself comfortable?" She disappeared into the bedroom, calling over her shoulder, "I'll just be a few minutes."

When she came back out, Derek was sprawled on her sofa, flipping channels on the TV. He smiled when she glided toward him. Rose to his feet. "I knew you were worth waiting for." Even as he admired the simple silver heart on a chain around her neck, he reached into his pocket and withdrew a slim velvet case. "And make no mistake, I have been waiting." He pressed it into her hand.

Eve's heart skipped a beat. Were they ready for this? She wasn't sure, but apparently he was. She drew a deep, enervating breath. "What is this?"

He let his gaze drift over her slowly, before looking back at her face. "Open it and see."

Fingers trembling slightly, she undid the ribbon. Inside was a beautiful garnet-and-platinum necklace, anchored by interlocking hearts. It wasn't overly expensive by Derek's financial standards, but it was gorgeous. She looked up at him. "What is this for?"

"The start of something wonderful," he said simply.

DEREK HAD KNOWN it was a gamble, giving a woman like Eve a gift. But he had wanted her to know she was special to him, and since she wouldn't let him say it, wouldn't believe him if he did, he'd contented himself with this symbol of togetherness.

Looking as if she wanted to say so much but couldn't, she drew in a jerky breath. "It's beautiful."

She removed the necklace she was wearing, and Derek helped her put the new one on. Eve sashayed over to the hall mirror with a rustle of shimmery silk, and checked out the effect.

"It really is perfect." She hesitated, showing the doubt he had expected from her all along. "Although I'm not entirely sure I should accept it," she finished softly.

Determined to win her over, no matter how long it took, Derek teased, "Consider it on loan, then. Until we officially start dating, that is."

Eve chuckled. "Confident, aren't you?"

"Absolutely," he fibbed. Placing his palm at her back, he walked her out the door and escorted her to his Jaguar. He opened her door for her and waited while she got in. Hand braced against the top of the car, he leaned in to drawl, "Now, when we get to the gala, are you going to be all business or just a little bit of business?"

Eve wrinkled her nose apologetically. "A lot business. It's a major opportunity for networking. I hope you don't mind."

He shook his head. "Not at all. As I mentioned the other day, I could do to expand my contacts here, too."

No sooner had they walked into the ball than they each spotted people they knew: Derek's brother Grady, and his wife, Alexis, and the architect that Eve had been playing phone tag with the past few days.

"Would you mind if I went to speak with Santiago Florres first?" she asked.

Derek gave his brother and sister-in-law the "one minute" sign, then leaned down and whispered in Eve's ear, "No problem. I'll go with you."

With his hand at her spine, he escorted her through the crowd of elegantly dressed guests to the line queuing up at the bar. Eve made the approach as graciously as always. "Mr. Florres? Eve Loughlin, Loughlin Realty." The two shook hands.

The architect, an affable-looking man in his late forties, got straight to the point. "I'm sorry I haven't returned your calls, Eve, but frankly, after I heard what Red Bloom offered for the home I designed, I wasn't sure what the two of us might have to say."

She nodded empathetically. "I'm aware it was insulting."

"Very." Santiago looked tense.

"I think," she continued, "that Mr. Bloom did not understand just how unique the home is."

The architect shrugged. "What does that have to do with me?" he snapped.

"A lot, actually." Her skill as a Realtor in full force, Eve smiled. "I think Mr. Bloom might change his mind about the value of the home currently for sale if you were to meet him and go through it with him, pointing out all the architectural features in that particular design that cannot be found anywhere else."

Derek noted that Florres's hostility had faded; the architect was now listening intently.

"Of course, if that should happen," Eve continued, "if a deal were to be made, then that would likely inflate the price of what you could charge for future architectural designs."

Florres considered that. Clearly, he felt his reputation had been harmed by the low offer. He moved nearer. "You're saying Mr. Bloom wants to meet with me?"

Eve lifted a hand. "I'm still trying to reach him, but if I can get something set up, would you be amenable?"

Santiago nodded with a mixture of relief and interest. "Yes, I would. And thanks, Eve, for giving me a chance to defend my work."

She handed him her business card. "I'll be in touch."

After chatting for a few more minutes, Derek and Eve walked off. She sighed. "Now all I have to do is get Red Bloom to come back to the house for another look, and I'll be all set."

Derek paused, not sure he'd heard her right. "Red Bloom, the Houston oilman?" he asked in surprise. That was the guy Marjorie and Eve had been chasing?

Eve nodded, distracted. She went on to refresh Derek's memory. "He is the client who amasses unique houses the way others collect fine art."

Derek slid a hand beneath her elbow and gave her a sidelong glance. "Do you anticipate having a problem getting Bloom to cooperate with your plan?"

She shrugged, then smiled at a colleague who caught her eye from across the room. "No way to say. To be perfectly honest, I haven't had any luck getting him on the phone."

Derek was about to suggest a solution to that when Eve stopped in her tracks. Looking abruptly ill at ease, she elbowed him gently. "There's your brother and his wife."

Hoping this meeting would go better than the first encounter between Eve and his siblings, Derek wrapped his arm around her waist and pulled her close as Grady and Alexis came toward them.

"I'M GLAD WE have a moment to talk," Alexis told Eve sincerely, after the two men had gone off to get champagne. "I want to apologize for what you overheard that weekend at the house. Derek's brothers were razzing him about his crush on you, so he pretended it was nothing, the way guys do. Which is when you showed up."

Embarrassed, Eve felt heat rise to her cheeks. Derek wasn't the only one with a crush. "It's okay."

"I figured Derek would make it up to you." Alexis's gaze drifted to the jewelry around Eve's neck. "If that necklace is as new as I think it is, I see that he has."

Eve's hand flew to her throat. She felt even more embarrassed now, probably because whatever it was that they had was too new and fragile to stand up to scrutiny.

Wondering if the veteran matchmaker thought she and Derek would last much beyond the holidays, which were admittedly a popular time for fleeting hookups, Eve asked, "How did you know this was from him?"

"Because he's my brother-in-law, and I know him." Alexis grinned. "Even when he was trying to convince us that the two of you weren't an item, for privacy's sake, I had the sense it was more than that. And this necklace proves it."

"I don't understand."

Gently, Alexis explained, "It's a McCabe thing. All the men buy the women jewelry when they are getting serious."

Eve wasn't sure whether to be elated or nervous. The only thing she knew for certain was that once again things seemed to be moving way too fast.

Luckily for her, the rest of the evening flew by. She and Derek both did a fair amount of networking, together and apart. And it was only when Derek was walking her to her front door that the conversation became truly intimate again. "Did Alexis say something to you tonight?"

Eve had been afraid this would come up. She fished her key from her bag and unlocked the door. Well after midnight, the condominium was blissfully quiet and still. "Why would you think that?" Derek shrugged and followed her inside. He undid his black bow tie and slipped it into the pocket of his tux. "Just a sense I had when my brother and I got back to the table. You had a funny look on your face." He peered at her. "In fact, it's still there."

"It's nothing."

He helped her remove her wrap, looking confident as ever. "It's something. Otherwise, you wouldn't still be so pensive."

She started to turn away, but found she couldn't. "Alexis thinks the fact you bought me a necklace is significant."

"And that upsets you?" he asked huskily, inching closer.

His voice washed over her, warming her from the inside out. "Is it significant?" Eve pressed.

Derek moved closer still and took her in his arms. "This," he said, lowering his lips to hers for a deep soulful kiss, "is significant. This…" he backed her toward her bedroom, leaving a trail of hot, fevered kisses over her throat, shoulder, breast "…is what we should be concentrating on."

Yearning swept through her, as powerful as the sensations his mouth and hands were generating. Eve curled her fingers in the fabric of his suit jacket. "Sex doesn't solve anything."

Derek bent her backward from the waist. "It doesn't

have to." Draping her over his arm, he kissed her again. "It's a wonder in and of itself."

Eve had to admit, as they undressed each other slowly and carefully, that he was right.

There was something incredible about being with him this way. Maybe it was the season. The fact she'd been alone too long, or he missed his daughter on the days and nights that Tiffany was with his ex and her new family. Or just the fact that he liked to say yes in his personal life whenever possible.

All Eve really knew was that when he kissed her and held her so intimately, the world narrowed to just the two of them and she felt treasured in that special man-woman way. And even if love wasn't involved, everything else that mattered was.

He was gentle and kind, and tender beyond measure. More important still, they were becoming very good friends. The kind who would always be there for each other, she thought as they kissed passionately, and she surrendered to him all the more.

Able to feel how much Eve needed him, Derek lay down with her on the satin sheets. His own body throbbing, he kissed the hollow of her stomach and the soft insides of her thighs, then drifted lower still, to deliver the most ardent of kisses. Overcome with pleasure, her heart pounding in rhythm with his, she whispered, "Derek…"

Shifting position, she moved to explore him, too. Seducing him, urging him on, molding her body to his, until they were both on fire. It was all too much. He brought her upward, claiming her mouth, claiming her. She lifted her hips and then they were one, riding the wave, going deeper, more intimately still, and then she was his, really his. Not just for tonight, he thought, not just for the holidays, or until their mutual loneliness passed. But until they found a way to give each other everything, heart and soul.

Chapter Thirteen

Sasha greeted Eve at the office door on Thursday morning. "Red Bloom phoned, asking to speak to you. He'd like you to return his call right away."

Finally, Eve thought. "Thanks." She took the message, went into her office and shut the door.

He answered promptly. "I hear you've got Florres ready to meet with me," Red boomed.

Although she had no idea how the brash Houston oilman could possibly know this, Eve affirmed with customary zeal, "I do."

"I'm going to be in Dallas later this afternoon. Does three o'clock work for you?"

Hoping and praying she could get the architect there, too, Eve said, "Absolutely."

"See you at the house, then."

Luckily, Santiago Florres was free to meet them, too. Probably because he was eager to defend his reputation as a creative genius.

Eve got to the house first. Red Bloom arrived next, in a white Rolls Royce with a Christmas wreath attached to the front grill. He squared his dove-gray Stetson on his head and strode toward her, the edges of his cashmere coat flapping open as he moved. As soon as cursory greetings were exchanged, he said, "I'm afraid I owe you an apology. I had no idea you were a friend of the McCabes until I spoke with Derek this morning."

Of course. Not sure how she felt about Derek interfering in her business life, Eve smiled brightly and pretended this wasn't news to her. "The two of you spoke?"

Red nodded. "He emailed me late last evening, and we spoke first thing today." The edges of Red's mustache curled upward. "His mother and I go way back. I've known Derek and his brothers since they were kids. His dad, too. Derek told me what a great help you'd been to him and his little girl. Said I couldn't go wrong listening to you, or your mother, for that matter."

Eve fished the key to the lockbox from her handbag. "I'm glad to hear Derek was so happy with the service he received from our company."

Not so glad Derek had gone behind her back to lobby for her, but that was another matter, Eve thought. One that would be dealt with privately when she figured out if having him involved in every aspect of her life was a good or bad thing.

Trying not to feel overwhelmed in the way Derek always made her feel, Eve started up the walk, just as a third car pulled up at the curb. Red turned. "Santiago Florres?" he asked as the driver joined them on the sidewalk.

"One and the same." Santiago reached out and shook his hand.

Eve could see she'd been right. When face-to-face, the two gentlemen had entirely different attitudes toward one another.

Hoping this session would have a better ending than the last, Eve led the way to the front steps of the starkly angular contemporary home, and on inside.

An engrossing two hours later, Eve said goodbye

to both men and drove downtown to the McCabe Venture Capital office. Derek was in a meeting when she arrived. She elected to wait.

Eventually, he came out of a conference room. Smiling cordially, he shook hands with the group of techies he'd been talking with, all of whom were bearing Tech Wizard T-shirts. Eve guessed the young businessmen and women were part of the small percentage that Derek said yes to, because they looked as if they had just received serious encouragement.

Looking incredibly happy to see her, as well as incredibly attractive in a dark suit and tie, Derek motioned Eve into his private lair and shut the door behind them.

Derek pulled her into a brief hug. "This is a nice surprise."

Eve withdrew. Part of her knew she shouldn't have been surprised by what Derek had done. After all, the McCabes were known far and wide for their kindness and generosity. Which was maybe the reason she had kept Red Bloom's identity from him for so long. Because she had feared if he did know just who it was that was giving her and her mother so much trouble, Derek might interfere on her behalf, rather than let her solve her problems herself.

Eve draped her coat over a chair and set her shoulder bag down in front of it. "Guess who called me this morning?"

Derek gazed at her, his poker face intact.

Eve stalked closer, her footsteps muffled by the thick carpet. "Red Bloom."

If there was one thing her mother had taught her, from the time she was a little girl, it was the importance of being self-reliant. The key to personal strength, Marjorie had said time and time again, was independence.

Relying on others to support or defend you was the surest path to unhappiness.

Eve had seen enough divorces to know it was true.

When a woman gave up everything to marry a man and raise his children, it left her vulnerable in more than just a financial sense.

And it always started with a man rushing to the rescue.

"Ah, yes. Red Bloom." Derek pulled a couple water bottles from the glass-door refrigerator built into the bar. He handed her one and twisted the cap off his own.

Eve sat down in a chair a distance away. She crossed her legs at the knee. "Apparently, you did a hard sell on my behalf?"

He came around to lean against the front of his desk, facing her. "I may have forgotten to mention he's an old family friend."

Eve sensed that was as close to an apology as she was likely to get. Like most gallant men, Derek would not harbor any regret for rushing to help a lady "in need." Especially if that lady was intimately involved with him.

She attempted to untwist the cap on her bottle, only to find it…stuck. Sighing, she set it on her lap, unopened. "I could have gotten through to him on my own."

Derek's expression remained impassive. He took a slow sip of water.

"But you don't believe that." She tried again to open her own bottle, and failed.

Derek set his water aside and ambled closer. "I think eventually you would have found a way to get the two men together." Wordlessly, he took the bottle from her and did what she could not, with a single, easy twist. His eyes locked with hers, he handed her the chilled water, stepped back. "Although perhaps not before the end of the year."

Eve snorted and took a sip. The icy water cooled her dry throat, but didn't do the same for her temper.

Derek leaned against his sleek mahogany desk once again. "How did the meeting with Bloom and Florres go, by the way?"

Eve took another sip. "Wonderfully. When they left, Red was talking to Santiago about designing a summer home for him in Galveston."

"The place in Highland Park that your mother listed? What about that?"

Eve took another sip. Feeling unbearably restless, she got up and wandered to the window. Arms tucked against her waist, she looked out at the city she loved. "At the end of the day, the two men still disagreed about the price. Santiago thinks it is worth every penny. Red still feels because of the unique design in an area of mostly traditional homes, that he'd have a hard time selling it if he did pay top dollar. And Red, as you know, does not like to waste money." Eve pivoted back to Derek. "However, he does understand Santiago's approach to design now, so in that sense the meeting was definitely a plus."

Derek tossed his empty bottle in the trash. "I'm sorry." He walked toward her languidly. "I hoped it would lead to a deal so your firm could take top spot in the sales competition."

Eve leaned one shoulder against the window. The chill of the glass was a marked contrast to the heat of his gaze. "It's not your problem."

He leaned a shoulder against the window pane, too, a small distance apart. "Funny," he said, his response as carefully measured as her own, "sometimes, when I see you looking so down, I feel as though it is my problem."

Eve slid him a wry look. It was a good thing he didn't know how much the vulnerable part of her wanted to throw herself in his arms and let him take all her troubles away. "If we ever retake the lead, I want it to be because Loughlin Realty has earned it, not because my guy friend has pulled some strings on my behalf."

Her declaration hung between them for a long moment. "Is that what I am?" Derek asked finally, masculine challenge in his eyes. "A *guy friend?*"

Eve ignored the implication to his question. "You know what I mean," she said shortly.

Abruptly seeming to realize it wasn't a good idea to push her—about anything—Derek dipped his head in acquiescence. "I do, and I'm sorry if I overstepped my bounds. I hope you'll forgive me?"

What was it about this man that made him so irresistible to her? Eve couldn't say; she only knew it to be true.

Eve released the breath she had been unconsciously holding. "I do."

Derek smiled. "Still coming to help me and Tiffany celebrate our first evening in our new house tonight?"

That, she was looking forward to. "I wouldn't miss it," Eve replied. She paused again, aware all over again how much she would like to kiss him, then and there.

Realizing that they were still in his place of business, and should act accordingly, she stepped away and went to grab her coat and bag. "What time?"

He gave her another heart-stopping smile. "Seven-thirty."

EVE WAS STILL at the office, wrapping things up, when Derek called her. "Do you want the bad news first, or the even worse news?" he rasped.

With her cell phone cradled against her ear, Eve walked a stack of letters to be mailed out to Sasha's desk. "Hit me with both."

"There's something wrong with the HVAC. It's not working at all."

"Oh, Derek, no! Did you call the contractor?"

Weariness radiated in his low voice. "He was just here. He thinks there's a flaw in the electronic ignition. Because it's brand-new, he's demanding a whole new unit from the manufacturer, but it won't be here until Monday."

Eve felt for Derek.

"The really big problem is I already checked out of my hotel, and they can't take us back. They're booked solid through the holidays."

As would be the case at many of the area's finer hotels. Eve shut down her computer. "Where's Tiffany?"

"With me at the house. In her coat and hat."

It was such a chilly day already, with the temperature set to dive into the twenties by nightfall. Eve didn't even have to think what to do. "Come to my place. You can stay there."

Sasha turned to Eve in surprise.

Eve waved her off.

With relief in his voice, Derek asked, "You're sure?"

She shut the door to her office. "We were headed to your hometown tomorrow morning, anyway. This will make it easier to get an early start." It didn't have to mean anything.

"We'll be right over. And, Eve?" he rumbled softly. *"Thanks."*

"The two of you are getting close," Sasha remarked as Eve prepared to leave.

More than she felt comfortable with, that was for

sure. Still, she couldn't turn away a man and his child when they were in need. "I feel for him and Tiffany. That's all."

"Mmm-hmm." Again that raised eyebrow.

Okay, so she could have helped him find another hotel, on the spot. Or had him call his brother Grady. Or let Carleen and Craig, or even his own assistant, Alma May, help. Trying not to flush, Eve shrugged on her coat. "He did me a favor. I owe him one."

"Of course."

She hunted around for her shoulder bag and keys. She'd just had them! "And Mom's place is still empty, since she's in rehab. I can stay there, while he and Tiffany bunk at my place."

Sasha gave Eve a look that reminded Eve just how well they knew each other. "Be careful," Sasha warned. "I know you like Derek and Tiffany a lot."

"But what?" Eve demanded impatiently, sensing there was more.

Sasha frowned. "Playing house with a man and his baby is not the same as the real thing."

That wasn't what they were doing, Eve reassured herself as she walked out to her car. But somehow she couldn't quite make herself believe it.

To HER CHAGRIN, Derek had his own doubts, too. "Maybe this isn't such a good idea, after all," he said half an hour later.

Eve looked at the scowl on Tiffany's face, aware once again how little experience she'd had with young children, or really, children of any kind.

Her mother had always been urging her to grow up, quickly! Not take care of other people's offspring.

Eve reached for a tissue. Gently, she blotted Tiffany's

red, tearstained cheeks. The toddler studied her from beneath her fringe of thick wet lashes, as if silently beseeching her to do *something!* Eve just didn't know what. "It'll be fine," she said, smiling despite herself when Tiffany reached out and curled her fingers around one of Eve's.

Without warning, the little girl threw herself into her arms. Eve caught her and held her close.

Tiffany's lower lip rolled out. She looked to be on the verge of another sob. Watching, Derek shoved his hands through his hair. "She's been fussing since we left the house."

Eve walked Tiffany around her apartment, rubbing her back gently. "Has she had dinner?"

He nodded. "Carleen fed her before I picked her up."

The little girl let out another wail. A new wave of tears rolled down her face, silent ones this time, which made her distress all the more heartbreaking. "Does she want a bottle?" Eve asked.

Derek produced one from the diaper bag. Tiffany pushed it away with both hands, and let out another angry, impatient wail.

Eve began to feel a little edgy, too. "Maybe if Tiffany was able to get down and walk around a little bit. Explore."

Eve had already cleared everything not baby-friendly from her reach.

"It's worth a try," Derek agreed.

Eve set her down gently and knelt beside her.

Tiffany wailed.

"Oh, sweetheart," Eve attempted to comfort the adorable baby girl. To no avail.

Derek hunkered down, murmuring soft words of

comfort, too. That did not work, either. He eased off Tiffany's hat and coat. She cried even louder.

Derek exchanged baffled looks with Eve and picked Tiffany back up again.

The tears kept coming.

While Derek walked Tiffany back and forth, Eve went to get her teddy bear and blanket.

Those offered no solace, either. They tried sitting together on the sofa. This had pleased Tiffany in the past. Tonight, Tiffany pushed both Derek and Eve away from her. Determined to find a way to comfort her, even if she did not have a rocking chair to sit in, Eve stood. She gathered Tiffany in her arms and began to sway gently, back and forth. The motion lulled the child, but only temporarily. "You don't think she's getting sick or something, do you?"

Derek pressed the back of his hand to Tiffany's cheek. "She doesn't seem to have any fever." He looked at Eve. "What do you think?"

She gently touched Tiffany's cheek, too. He was right. It was wet from her tears, but not in the least bit hot.

Tiffany again pushed her father away. When he stepped back, she twisted and sobbed. "Daddy!" Eve handed the little girl back to him.

He paced the length of the condo living room, his baby in his arms. Eve went down a mental checklist of things that had pacified the child before. "Do you think she could need a diaper change?"

He shook his head. "I changed her before we came over. And there's no diaper rash or detergent allergy or anything that would be making her uncomfortable. So that's not it." He paused, thinking, walking back and forth. Tiffany sobbed louder. Derek looked over his daughter's halo of dark curls. "Maybe if we offered her a bottle again. Apple juice, this time."

Again, it was rejected after barely one sip.

Tiffany demanded Eve hold her again. Eve cradled her tenderly in her arms and walked the room, the same as Derek. The toddler fussed and squirmed and grabbed Eve's hair in both fists and wailed in what sounded like raw fury. Which Eve could kind of understand, since all of Tiffany's efforts to communicate with them had failed mightily. They had no more idea what was wrong now than they had when she'd arrived.

"This is really unlike her," Derek said, reaching over to try and wrestle strands of Eve's hair from Tiffany's little fists.

And that was when his little girl leaned over and bit his hand as hard as she possibly could.

Derek let out a muffled grunt of pain.

Tiffany stopped crying and looked up at him in satisfaction.

And suddenly, Derek and Eve both knew. "Could she be teething?" she asked.

Derek ran his thumb along Tiffany's gum. He pushed back her lip. There were two white teeth on the bottom, and another one coming in next to the two white teeth on top.

"No wonder," he murmured, looking at the red, swollen gum, with a tooth that was only just beginning to tear through the tissue.

Tiffany bit down again. Derek grunted in pain. His daughter smiled.

Eve chuckled. "Well, at least we know what to do now."

There was only one problem, as it turned out.

"Oh, no. I don't believe it. It's not in here," Derek

groaned. "I must have left the first-aid kit with the stuff at the house."

And, Eve knew, it was a thirty-minute drive there and back. "There's a drugstore on the corner," she said as Tiffany began to cry once again, softly this time.

Derek looked torn, but there was no doubt in either adult's mind what would be faster. "Is it okay if I leave her here with you while I go?"

"Sure."

The minute he walked out, Tiffany began to cry again, in great choking sobs. Having seen her swollen gum, Eve couldn't blame the child. "You know what?" she told Tiffany resolutely. "We're not going to wait for someone to rescue us. We're going to look for a solution ourselves."

Eve carried the tyke into the kitchen. She opened the freezer, intending to get ice. Then smiled when she saw an even better solution. "Tiffany, sweetheart, I think I have what we both need…."

DEREK HURRIED AS fast as he could. It was still twenty minutes before he got back to Eve's condo. He expected to hear Tiffany wailing up a storm. Instead, all was quiet. In fact, he observed as he opened the front door, there was only…*laughter?*

He rounded the corner and found Eve lounging on her overstuffed white sofa. Her shoes were off, her hair looked sticky and her gold silk blouse was smeared with something white. Tiffany was on her lap. Her hair was sticky, too. As were her hands and her face, and her clothes.

She was also smiling.

"More," Tiffany demanded happily, grinning from ear to ear.

"A gal after my own heart," Eve exclaimed, offering a tiny spoonful of what looked to be the last of a small carton of premium vanilla ice cream.

Derek came closer.

And in that instant, as he took in both the woman and his little girl, he knew. He wasn't just enamored of Eve. He didn't just want her as a friend, or a lover, or both.

He wanted her as his wife.

"ASLEEP AT LAST." Eve and Derek stood in the corner of the master bedroom, which was illuminated only by a night-light. Tiffany was curled up on her side in the port-a-crib, her teddy in her arms, her favorite blanket spread over top of her. She looked incredibly angelic and sweet.

Eve shook her head, thinking of what the little girl had been through that evening before she and Derek had figured out what the problem was. "Poor little thing," she whispered to Derek.

He wrapped his arm about her shoulders and pulled her in close. Bending down, his sandpapery beard brushing her temple, he pressed a kiss to her forehead before turning back to regard his daughter once again. "The combination of acetaminophen and numbing gel are working great at the moment, anyway."

Eve turned to face Derek. Together, they eased from the room, leaving the door open.

"And when it wears off four hours from now?" She couldn't help but worry about the little girl, the way a mom would. It had been heart-wrenching, seeing Tiffany so distressed.

Derek predicted, with the expertise of a very hands-on daddy, "She'll probably be up again. But don't worry...I'll handle it."

Eve wondered if this was what it would feel like if the three of them ever became a family. She only knew she didn't want to let this kind of happiness go, and that scared her. It was too soon to be thinking this way and wanting so much. Too soon to be risking so much of her heart...

Oblivious to the tumultuous nature of her thoughts, but sensing something was amiss, Derek studied her closely. "What's wrong?"

Eve shrugged and forced her mind back to the practical. "Well, for starters, I wish I had an actual guest bedroom."

Then the three of them could have all comfortably stayed there.

Instead, he was going to have to sleep in her room, in her bed, while she went elsewhere.

Derek ambled toward her. "Still planning to sleep at your mother's?"

Eve pushed the mental image of a half-naked Derek, lounging against her pillows, out of her head. She didn't need to know how he looked in her ultrafeminine satin bedcovers. And she certainly didn't need to be envisioning what it would be like to make love to him there. She swallowed around the sudden parched feeling in her throat and turned away from his probing gaze. "I thought you might like your privacy."

He shot her a bold, possessive look. "What I would like is to have you here."

She flushed and struggled to keep her guard up. "On the sofa?"

"Or in bed, with me. Where, just so you'll know, all we will do is sleep."

Eve knew that with Tiffany in there, everything in her bedroom would be totally G-rated. Oddly enough, the idea of bedding down with Derek—without hooking up—seemed even more fraught with peril. Cuddling all night, just for the sake of cuddling, was the kind of thing that could entice one to fall in love. And given how very close she was to that, as it was...

She turned toward him, drew a breath of the bracing scent of his hair and skin, and tried not to fall any harder for him. "Are you sure my place isn't too small for the three of us?"

Derek didn't seem the least bit discomfited by the physical or emotional intimacy of such an arrangement. He met her eyes and didn't look away. "Actually, it's just right for one night." He favored her with a brief, warm smile. "Although I have to wonder..." He paused, slightly perplexed. "Given your success as a real estate broker, why don't you have a bigger place?"

Good question. And one she had been asked before.

Eve went into the kitchen. She opened the drawer where she kept several take-out menus and pulled out a stack. "It's the reality of my business." She fanned the menus across the counter so he could choose one, then turned to face him again. "Real estate is among the hardest-hit business in any economic downturn. When that happens, commissions can be few and far between. So, as a hedge against that, my mother and I both live way beneath our means."

Derek bypassed the dinner selection process and instead made himself comfortable, lounging against the counter next to her, watching her. "Nothing wrong with being cautious financially," he murmured, "so long as you're emboldened to take risks in other aspects of your life."

Risks, Eve noted, that seemed to include whatever this was with him. Her heart stilled and she wet her lips, aware that with Tiffany sleeping on the other side of the apartment, anything could happen here. "I thought this was going to be a G-rated evening." He moved so that she was between him and the counter, and braced a hand on either side, trapping her against his long, hard length. He bent to nuzzle the sensitive side of her neck. "In the bedroom." He found his way to her ear, her throat, then eventually her mouth. "We're not there now," he whispered, expertly fitting his lips to hers. He stopped and grinned. "We're in the kitchen."

And the kitchen suddenly seemed a very erotic place to be. Eve groaned, even as her arms went up to wreathe his shoulders. Before she knew it, she was kissing him back. "You make a tempting case."

"And you are one tempting woman." He nuzzled his way down to the first button of her blouse. "Even with ice cream in your hair."

Eve touched a hand to the stickiness she had entirely forgotten about. He was right; several strands were matted with vanilla ice cream. "Ohhh."

He threaded his fingers through her hair and then bent and kissed her temple, then her cheek. "You're one hell of a good woman, Eve," he whispered as his mouth drifted slowly toward hers. "Do you know that?"

She pulled him flush against her and opened her lips to the investigating pressure of his. She moaned again, her entire body going soft with pleasure. He kissed her again, a deep, giving kiss that had her senses spinning and her heart soaring. "I know you make me feel that way."

They kissed again, even more passionately, holding nothing back, seeking solace in the harbor of each other's arms. "And I know you're one hell of a good man,"

Eve told him breathlessly, undoing the buttons of his shirt while he made short work of hers.

Derek grinned as both garments fell to the ground. His undershirt went the same way as her bra. As the heat and strength of his erection pressed against her, he cupped the weight of her breasts in his hands, rubbed his thumbs across her taut nipples. "Always something to be said for being on the same page."

Seemingly in no hurry, he lowered his lips to hers again. Eve kissed him back, sweetly and reverently. She ran her palms across the width of his shoulders, down his spine, luxuriating in the satiny feel of his skin and the flex of masculine muscle, aware that nothing had ever seemed as right as this.

Derek hadn't come there with the idea of making love to Eve. Given the way the evening had started out, he hadn't expected to have any opportunity to show her how much he cared for her. But now that the moment was here, he wasn't going to walk away without giving free rein to the primal possessiveness that emerged every time he was near her.

He kissed his way down her body, easing open the zipper of her skirt. Soon she was wearing nothing but a sparkly golden thong.

And eventually that went, too. Nudging her legs apart, he settled between her open thighs, sliding even lower. Eve gasped as his mouth crossed the flat of her abdomen. And she caught his head between her trembling palms when he went lower still, lifting her against his kisses, circling and retreating, adoring, seducing, until at last she fell apart in his hands. Satisfaction roared through him when he heard her choppy breathing and the sexy sounds being ripped from her throat. He held her until the last of her shudders had passed, then moved upward once again. In a flash, whatever clothes remained were off.

And then it was her turn to fulfill his fantasies. Kissing and touching, wrapping her hands around his thighs before sending him into a frenzy of wanting, of need.

He urged her upward. She shifted. Once again their eyes locked, their lips met, and then he was lifting her onto the counter, pulling her to the edge and stepping in. Luxuriating in the hot, intense quality of their connection, he penetrated her slowly, then caught her by the hips and let her do for him, with the most feminine part of her, what he had already done for her. Eve moaned and melded into him, murmuring his name again and again. Already granite-hard, he rocked against her and took his time, going ever deeper, slower, demanding she surrender to him completely.

And she did. Heaven help him, she did, until there was no more blood left in his head. Until there was no more prolonging the inevitable, no more holding their passion and their feelings in check, and the two of them went spiraling over the edge, still kissing, still clutching each other, still giving one another everything it was possible to give.

And then some, he realized shakily, as they clung together through the aftershocks. Affirming, to him and to her, that however this had started, their coming together was a hell of a lot more than just sex. It was, he thought, what she was to him, and he was to her: the best Christmas gift ever.

Chapter Fourteen

Eve's phone rang at seven o'clock the next morning. She was not surprised to see her mother's caller ID pop up on screen. Marjorie wasted no time on preambles. "Have you seen this morning's newspaper?"

"No." Careful not to wake Derek and Tiffany, who were both still sleeping, Eve slid a robe on over her silk pajamas and popped out to get it.

"Check the business section."

Front page was a banner headline: Sibley & Smith Leading Year End Real Estate Sales Race.

Eve groaned. "I'm sorry, Mom."

"Not that one. Loughlin Realty is not about to let that one stand, at least not for the long haul."

Eve imagined when her mother got back to work, things would be different. Marjorie's enthusiasm for the business was always contagious. When she was around, sales were made and deals were closed almost effortlessly, it seemed.

"Farther down the page," Marjorie instructed with her usual zeal. "Next to a photo of someone familiar."

On the lower half was a picture of Derek beside an impressively long article. Eve read aloud, "'McCabe Venture Capital funds Tech Wizard, the next big thing in entertainment streaming and information. Expected to outperform everything currently available…'" Eve quickly scanned the remainder of the story. "Wow." And she thought he was successful now.

"So," Marjorie continued, business as usual, "you should have no problem selling him another property—or even two—before the end of the year, given the money he had originally budgeted and expected to spend." Behind her, Eve heard a gleeful, high-pitched shriek, and pivoted to see Tiffany toddling toward her. Her fluffy dark curls smashed to her head and going every which way, her cheeks pink with sleep, she ran toward Eve, arms outstretched. "Mommy!" she yelled with familiar affection. "Mommy!"

Eve heard a gasp on the other end of the connection. "What is that?" Marjorie pressed. "Or maybe I should say, *who* is that?"

Tiffany grinned at Eve, showing the new tooth that had broken through her gum overnight. She knelt down to hug the child and mugged back at her wordlessly. "Um, a friend," she told her mom.

"Me!" Tiffany grabbed for the phone. "'Lo!" she squealed into the receiver.

Derek intercepted his daughter, swinging her quickly into his arms with a theatrical effect that made her giggle uproariously. Mouthing *"Sorry!"* to Eve, he handed Tiffany his phone to talk on.

She threw it down. The cell phone bounced as it hit Eve's thick, luxurious carpeting. "Bottle!" Tiffany yelled. "Me! Bottle!"

Waggling her brows at Derek, Eve pointed to the fridge and stepped away from where he was heading, baby daughter in tow.

"Since when do you pal around people with babies

at seven in the morning? Unless…" Marjorie paused thoughtfully "…you had an overnight guest?"

Unwilling to respond to that, Eve flushed. Her mother would approve of her using everything she had to leverage a sale with Derek. She would not, however, approve of her sleeping with him.

Eve turned and made her way toward her bedroom. A look at the rumpled covers only brought back more memories. Of how it had felt to sleep, fully clothed, wrapped in his arms. She turned toward the living room, only to be reminded of all they had done before they'd headed off to sleep. With her body tingling erotically, she shoved a hand through her tousled hair. "Mom, I have to go."

"Are you still going to Laramie today to look at property with Derek McCabe?"

"Yes." Eve swallowed, trying to get a hold of herself, to sound at least vaguely normal. "But if you need me here, Mom…"

"I need you to make a big sale, Eve. Enough to put us in the lead of the sales race again."

Eve glanced again at the front page of the business section and the stories on her family's business versus Derek's. There was no doubt whose money-generating venture was going better. No doubt about who juggled work and family more effectively.

"I know you can get emotional about property, and the needs and wants of the people buying it, but there's no time for that. Promise me you'll pull this off for us," Marjorie insisted.

Eve rubbed her temples. If her mother wasn't currently recovering from a heart attack, they'd be having a different conversation. One a lot more frank, about Eve's need to start separating her professional life from her personal one, her need to have her own life. Before Derek and Tiffany had come into her world, Eve realized, she hadn't done anything but work, and worry about work. In retrospect, it was not a satisfying way to live.

As much as she wanted to please her mother, Eve didn't want to lose what precious little balance she had already found. "I'll do my best to see that Derek and his little girl get what they need today, Mom," she promised.

Picking up on Eve's reluctance, Marjorie sighed. "I'm sorry I'm pushing, but to see everything we've all worked so hard for this year end on a whimper instead of a bang... It's disheartening."

What an apt phrase, Eve thought. "I know, Mom. I wish..." What did she wish? That she'd already sold all three properties and put them firmly in the lead for the year? Or that she didn't have to worry so much about whether she was ambitious enough to please her mom, and could instead concentrate on trying to make some sort of satisfying home life for herself that included more than just the two of them? There was a choked sound on the other end of the connection. "Oh, honey. I'm sorry," her mother said abruptly. "Forget all that." Sounding more like the new and improved, post-heart attack Marjorie than the previous go-getter, she continued emotionally, "It's you I care about, Eve. And your happiness."

"I know, Mom," she said.

She knew her mother was struggling to find balance in her life, too. To do what she needed for her health, and yet not neglect the business she'd spent her life building.

Still, old habits died hard. And Eve felt the weight

of her mother's expectations like an anchor around her neck.

When she ended the call, Derek was watching her.

He was clad in low-slung pajama pants, and nothing else. With the shadow of a beard on his face, his hair rumpled, his eyes intent, his daughter still cradled in his arms, he was sexy as all get-out. Their eyes met. Her heart took a little leap, and deep within her, desire built.

"Everything okay?" His tone was a seductive rumble. Caring. Protective.

Eve didn't want to talk about anything that would ruin what they had shared the evening before. "You're famous!" She pointed to the business section of the paper.

Derek ignored his own photo and what for him was old news. He frowned. "Sorry about that." He tapped the Sibley & Smith story. "But as they say, it's not over till it's over. And there are still eleven days left in the year."

Yes, there were. And Eve didn't want to talk about that, either. Fearing the end of Christmas would mean the end of their romance, she walked past him into the kitchen. "What do the two of you want for breakfast?"

He set Tiffany down on the floor. She toddled toward the small carryall of toys they'd brought with them, and sat down happily to play.

Derek followed Eve around the other side of the breakfast bar that divided the two rooms. He moved the curtain of her hair and nuzzled her neck just below her ear. "How about something soft and hot…." he whispered, conjuring up images of what they'd done the night before.

Eve turned, poker-faced. "Cream of Wheat?"

He laughed, seemingly content to wait until the right

time to put the moves on her again. Playfully, she tapped a finger to her chin. "Or oatmeal?"

He gave her another look that let her know she wasn't going to be able to resist him if he was around for long, and it appeared he intended to be around for quite a while.

Eve swallowed, beginning to feel overwhelmed again. "Seriously…"

He looked in her fridge, saw the loaf of bread, butter, eggs and jam. Then turned back to her, obviously ready and willing to do whatever it took to make her feel better. "How about," he drawled sexily, "you let me make breakfast?"

And he could cook, too. Really, Eve thought with a wistful sigh, what was *not* to love about this man?

"So WHAT'D YOU think of the Double H ranch, now that you've had a chance to see it again?" Josie McCabe asked Derek when they got back from their tour of the property.

Derek grinned at his mom. "Same as I recall."

"Another fixer-upper?" his brother Colt teased, referring to the broken-down house and barns that, thanks to the family who owned it and didn't reside there, hadn't seen much in the way of upkeep in many a year.

Derek grinned at him, too, as recklessly sentimental as ever when it came to choosing real estate. "I prefer to think of it as in need of some tender loving care."

"What'd you think, Eve?" Wade asked.

"It's very picturesque," she said sincerely. The five-thousand-acre ranch seemed to have everything, from tree-lined streams and rocky bluffs to flat, sagebrush-dotted plains.

"Not to mention remote," Derek's older brother, Grady, remarked.

Josie scowled. "Well, anything in Laramie County fits that description."

Derek agreed with his mom. "Nothing wrong with remote," he drawled.

"Unless you've lived your whole life in a big city like Dallas," Grady said, with a brief, telling look at Eve. "Then it can seem like wilderness."

No kidding, Eve thought. During the three-and-a-half-hour drive to Laramie County, there had been long stretches of highway without a gas station or town to be found. Never mind any cell phone reception, which had made responding to work emails and client texts challenging, to say the least.

"Well, I for one will be happy to have you-all close again, at least part of the time," Josie said, hugging first Derek, then her granddaughter. She held her arms wide and embraced Eve warmly. "You, too, hon." They drew apart. "In the meantime, we better do something about dinner."

A mixture of laughs and groans immediately followed. Josie took the good-natured ribbing about her culinary talents in stride. Apparently, Eve noted, being in the kitchen was one of Josie McCabe's least favorite things. Hence, she was happy to turn the cooking over to others. "Mom, you're in charge of the three grandkids," Derek declared.

Josie winked at him. "As long as you and Colt stay to help corral them."

Wade headed for the flagstone patio. "I'll fire up the grill."

"We'll help you." Grady, Justin and Rand followed their dad.

Amanda, Alexis and Shelley—the three women who had married into the family—headed for the kitchen. "Not to worry, Josie. We'll take care of everything in here." Wanting to be of some help, Eve followed suit.

The kitchen, like everything else in the sprawling ranch house, was designed for a big family. There were two Sub-Zero refrigerators, two dishwashers, two sinks, a wide kitchen island that spanned the length of the long room and an abundance of windows to look out, and counters on which to work.

In short order, vegetables were brought out to be cleaned and cooked, fruits peeled and sliced, the meats seasoned and prepared for the grill.

Finally, enough prep work had been done to allow a respite. A round of long-necked bottles of Texas-brewed beer was opened and passed out. Conversation ensued about people and places Eve knew nothing about. Not sure where she fit in, or *if* she fit in, she hung back.

Noticing her unease, the six-foot-tall Amanda came over to give her a comforting hug. "Hey. No need to be panicked here. We're all friends."

Eve could see that.

Alexis stopped what she was doing and came over to give Eve's hand a squeeze.

Shelley comforted her with a smile. "The three of us are all only children. I grew up here and dated Colt when we were teens, so I already knew his family. It didn't matter how nice they were to me. They intimidated me for years—until I let them in."

Amanda nodded in agreement. "I got to know Justin and his dad when I was working on the boys' ranch that Justin founded. They made me feel like family from the outset, but I was still intimidated the first time I came to Josie and Wade's ranch to be with everyone."

"Me, too," Alexis recounted with a shake of her head. "As much as Grady tried to prepare me, I was still overwhelmed my first visit here when I saw everyone together."

So it wasn't just her, Eve thought.

She wondered why it didn't help to know that.

"It will get better with time," Amanda soothed, with the knowledge of a woman who had been there, and not only survived, but thrived. "Just relax and soak it all in."

Amazed, and a little disconcerted by how quickly they had accepted her into the tribe and made her feel like part of the family, Eve hugged each of the three women in turn.

Yet as much as she wanted to, she knew she couldn't get used to this, or in any way take it for granted. It didn't matter how much she longed to step into such a Texas-style perfect life. Or how much Derek and his family seemed to want it all to be a done deal.

It was much too soon for that.

THE REST OF the weekend passed quickly. Derek wasn't surprised to see Eve getting along well with his family. They were, perhaps, more alike than she knew. He also realized that something was bothering her, and had been since they'd looked at the rural property the previous day. Wanting to talk to her about it without interruption, however, he waited until he had dropped Tiffany at Carleen's house and taken Eve back to hers.

"You've been awfully quiet," he said, carrying her suitcase into her condo. Except for the phone call she'd made to her mother en route, she hadn't spoken much on the drive back to Dallas, and instead had contented herself watching the scenery and listening to Christmas carols on the car stereo.

Eve gave him a wan smile. There was a sadness in her eyes he didn't like. "I was trying to figure out how to talk to you about the Double H ranch."

Derek took off his coat and sat down on the sofa. "I'm listening."

Instead of taking the seat beside him, Eve settled into an armchair opposite. "You also know I'm not the kind of Realtor who is all about the commissions."

Derek got serious, too. "You like to match the right property with the right person."

Eve affirmed this with a decisive nod. "I know what your financial goals are, in terms of investing in real estate before the end of the year. There is still time for them to be met."

Derek braced himself for the bad news sure to come. "Are you trying to say you didn't like the ranch I showed you?" he asked, searching her eyes. "Because if that's the case, we can go back to Laramie County, keep looking."

Her soft lips took on a grim line. "I don't think you understand, Derek. My likes and my dislikes don't enter into this transaction."

What was she talking about? "Of course they do!"

"Not in the way you seem to be thinking," she countered in a tight, controlled voice.

He forced himself to show no reaction. Although this wasn't what he wanted to hear—not by a long shot—part of him had always figured it would come to this. Eve was simply not a woman who wanted to let anyone in.

"Are you breaking up with me?" he asked quietly.

Still holding his eyes—even more reluctantly now, he noticed—she cleared her throat. "Derek, we're not even dating."

He stood, hands braced on his waist. "Right. We're just sharing confidences and spending time together and making love with each other every chance we get."

Pink color flooding her cheeks, Eve stood, too. "Your family pretty much has us married off!"

Derek strode nearer, positioning himself so she had no choice but to look at him. Hands on her shoulders, he held her in front of him when she would have run. "That's because they know the two of us are made for each other," he said gruffly.

Tears misted Eve's pretty amber eyes. "You can't know that."

Aware of all that was at stake here—their future happiness—he held his ground. "I do know that."

Her tears spilled down her cheeks. She pulled away from him. "Well, I don't."

He watched her pace to the window, then stand there as if she had the weight of the world on her shoulders. "What are you saying?"

She pivoted back around to face him, looking edgy and upset. "I'm saying I know how, once you make up your mind about something—like buying a home or vacation retreat— that you just want to find a way to get it done. Ideally, as fast as possible."

It wasn't the first time Derek's success and determination had been held against him, but it had never hurt this much before.

She gazed into his eyes, a soul-deep weariness in her expression. "With that in mind, I know how determined you are to make sure that your little girl has parity in her two homes, so that she doesn't suffer because she comes from divorced parents." Eve drew in an uneven breath. "And I know that Tiffany wants a mommy and a daddy at both of her houses, that the three of us work well as a team, and that Tiffany adores me as much as I adore her."

She was making their connection sound so cold and calculated. "You think I made love with you because I need a bed buddy, and a friend, and I want you to be a mother to my child?"

"No." Eve's eyes were steady, but her lower lip trembled. "I think you made love to me because it's Christmastime and you want someone to celebrate with…and you find me as wildly attractive as I find you. I think you want me because it's easier to have two people parent a child at any given time than just one."

What about heart? Didn't that come into all this? His? Hers? In her view, Derek realized, it apparently did not. Hurt beyond measure, he stared at her. "But you don't want a future with me, is that it?" How could he have been so wrong about her, about all of this?

A shadow of regret crossed her face. "I'm saying what I've been saying all along—that I don't feel comfortable rushing into anything, Derek." She wrung her hands together. "And the truth of the matter is we have rushed into this, for a lot of reasons, none of them good."

Derek reached out and caught her by the waist when she would have moved away. "Okay, you've told me my reasons. As you see them, anyway," he amended brusquely, stung by the look in her eyes. "What are yours?"

She threw up her hands. "My mother had a heart attack and that made me realize how short life is, and how one-dimensionally I've been living." Raw emotion filled Eve's voice. "The crisis made me want comfort, and it made me want a lot more than I've had."

She deserved a whole hell of a lot more, too. Derek

drew her against him and tucked a strand of hair behind her ear. "I want more, too," he confessed. *"I want you."*

She splayed her hands over his chest, still holding him at bay. "There were other reasons, too." Her voice sounded thick with unshed tears. "I told you that I get depressed and lonely around the holidays. That I never ever felt like I could quite get into the Christmas spirit the way others did." She paused, her teeth raking across her delectably soft lower lip. "Reaching out to you and Tiffany and celebrating the season with you made all of that go away."

For him, too.

But for him it had been just the beginning.

For Eve, it seemed it was the end. And that scared Derek more than he wanted to admit. "And that's all our love affair was?" he prodded, desperately wanting her to rise up angrily and tell him otherwise. "A temporary reprieve from a family crisis and some scary, uncomfortable feelings?"

Eve paused. She started to say something, stopped. She pushed away from him entirely and ran a hand through her hair. "I don't know if that's what it was or not," she said brokenly. The tortured words came straight from her heart. "I don't know *what* we are to each other. Or how we'll even feel once the holidays pass, and you and Tiffany settle in at your place. Which is why...I want to take a break."

"Now," he repeated, when she still refused to look him in the eye. "Four days before *Christmas?*"

Another nod. A sigh. And this time she did look at him, as calm, cool and collected as the day they'd first met. "For at least a month, Derek. Maybe two."

And then what? he wondered. Did she honestly think this would hurt them any less if they delayed the inevitable? He folded his arms in front of him, legs braced apart. "No."

Eve blinked, obviously as unprepared for his reaction as he had been for hers. "What?" she asked, as if she couldn't possibly have heard him right.

"I'm not going to go through some arbitrary time-out," he told her flatly. Hurt and disappointed beyond measure, he stepped closer and stared down at the beautiful woman he adored so much, the woman he had foolishly hoped he would spend the rest of his life with.

He had wanted Eve to feel as he did, that they were made for each other.

Clearly, she didn't. And if that was the case, he'd already been down this particular road. He damn well wasn't traveling it again.

Aware that she was still staring at him in shock, he exhaled wearily, then forced himself to go on in a matter-of-fact tone. "If you don't already know that you and I are the best thing that ever happened to each other, then you're never going to know, Eve. And I can't—won't—be part of another relationship where I'm the only one ready and willing to put my whole heart in, and give it my all."

"You're breaking up with me?" she asked, aghast, looking as if this possibility hadn't ever occurred to her.

Derek grabbed his coat and headed for the door. He didn't want to end it, but he didn't want to prolong the pain, either. He nodded curtly. "You've given me no choice."

Chapter Fifteen

Eve spent most of Sunday night crying her eyes out. Monday morning was just as bad. And it got worse when she received the latest news on the real estate front.

Reluctantly, she went to see her mother and tell her in person.

"The offer on Flash's condo fell through."

Marjorie didn't look surprised.

Eve swept a hand through her hair. "There are no other bids. And probably won't be until after the holidays."

Her mom nodded slowly. She put down the novel she had been reading. "The Santiago Florres–designed house?"

The ache of defeat grew. "Red is passing on it. He is, however, in negotiations with Santiago to build him something just as unique on the beach in Galveston. Unfortunately, there's no chance we'll see a commission there, either. Their lawyers will be brokering that deal."

Marjorie pursed her lips, looking surprisingly calm. "Anything else?"

Eve gulped. And here was the worst part, as far as business was concerned, anyway. She looked her mother straight in the eye. "Sibley & Smith sold another four-million-dollar listing over the weekend."

"So in other words, they've won."

Eve went and perched on the edge of her mother's bed. "Unless someone takes over the negotiations on a property for Derek McCabe."

Her mom rose and went to the mini-fridge next to the sink. "Why can't you do it?"

For so many reasons, Eve thought. Most of which were currently breaking her heart. She clenched her hands on either side of her. "It's complicated."

Marjorie passed Eve a can of low-sodium tomato juice and kept one for herself. "Fortunately, I'm in cardiac rehab, so I have all the time in the world when I'm not down in physical therapy, working on regaining my strength." She smiled wryly at her daughter. "So give it to me straight."

Eve looked down as she popped the top on her drink. "I got too involved."

Marjorie sat down next to her on the hospital bed. "Too involved or not enough?"

Eve gave in to the need to be comforted, and rested her head on her mother's shoulder. "He wanted things from me, Mom, that I'm just not cut out to give."

Marjorie wrapped her arm about her shoulders and pulled her in close, the way she had when Eve was a little girl. "Things like what?" she asked gently.

Eve swallowed a lump in her throat. "Marriage."

"He proposed?"

She straightened, took a drink. "No."

Marjorie moved so they were facing each other, then studied her with a mother's knowing eye. "Then…?"

Eve flushed and took another sip of the sweet, mellow juice. "We were headed in that direction."

"Since when is that a bad thing?"

Barely able to believe she'd said that, Eve blinked. "You've never wanted to get married, Mom!"

"So?" Marjorie shrugged. "I'm not you." After a short pause, she said, "It has to be more than that."

Eve lurched to her feet. "Everything was just happening way too fast." As usual when upset, she started to pace.

Marjorie shifted back against the pillows. "Sometimes life is that way."

Eve had expected her to take her side in this! Whirling toward her mom, she said stubbornly, "I wanted a break. He wouldn't give it to me."

"Hmm."

Once again, hurt mixed with disbelief. Eve scoffed. "That's it? That's all you have to say?"

Marjorie finished her juice and set the container aside. "What do you want me to say?"

That was just it…Eve didn't know. She shook her head miserably. "Something to make me feel better!"

Marjorie smiled sympathetically. "I don't think I can do that, honey."

"You always have before."

"You were never really and truly this—"

Eve expected her mom to say "wildly infatuated before."

Instead, she said, "—foolish before."

It was Eve's turn to study her mother, long and hard. "I know he's well-off financially, Mom. I know he's phenomenally successful, professionally. But just because everything is easy for him doesn't mean it's going to be easy for me, never mind easy for us."

Her inscrutable demeanor fading, her mother nodded sagely. "Especially if you do everything you can to make it more difficult than it has to be."

Honestly! "Whose side are you on?" Eve demanded angrily.

Her mother replied flatly, "Yours."

It sure didn't seem like that was the case. Eve squared her shoulders and regarded her defiantly, aware they hadn't been this far apart in anything since her teenage years. "Maybe we shouldn't talk about this."

Surprisingly, her mother agreed. "It does seem like you need to do a little more soul-searching." Marjorie rose and guided Eve toward the door. She gave her a long, heartfelt hug. "But I have faith that, given enough time and solitude, you'll figure it out."

ACUTELY AWARE THIS was the last place he had expected to be at noon on December 23, Derek stood in the doorway of Marjorie Loughlin's room. He didn't know Eve's mother all that well yet. He also didn't know where else to go for help in, if not making things right, at least trying to make amends. He drew a breath. "Got a minute?"

Marjorie put down the crossword puzzle she'd been working on. She removed her glasses and looked down her nose at him. "For you? I'm not sure, given that you've broken my daughter's heart."

"Hey." Derek lifted both hands defensively. "She's the one who refused to get serious about me." He was the one who had wanted an enduring relationship. Not in the distant future, but right now. "She is the one who kept saying no."

The older woman quirked her lips. "Maybe for good reason, since she says the two of you were never even dating."

Derek sauntered in. He pulled up a chair and got

comfortable. "And if you believe that, I've got some swampland in East Texas to sell you."

Marjorie grinned and began to relax. "Why are you here?"

He sobered. "I want help buying enough property to help Loughlin Realty win the sales competition."

A long, suspenseful moment passed. "Why?"

"Because it's Christmas, a time of giving, and it means something to Eve," Derek informed her. "And because I feel I owe her that much."

"For?"

This was tricky. "Hurting her without meaning to." *Hurting us both by pushing her too hard, too fast.*

"Balderdash." Marjorie stood abruptly.

Derek got to his feet, too. "Excuse me?"

The woman stomped closer, at that moment looking a lot like her beautiful, tempestuous daughter. "What a load of hooey."

Like hell it was.

Derek faced off with Marjorie. "Eve wants to win that sales race."

With a shake of her head, her mom corrected, "*Wanted* to win. For me. I told her it wasn't necessary. There's always next year."

Derek blinked in disbelief.

Marjorie shrugged. "Three and a half weeks of cardiac rehab will make a person examine what does and does not make him or her happy. For me, it's a successful business, always has been, always will be. For Eve, it's a lot more complicated." Marjorie wandered over to adjust the holiday wreath affixed to her wall before turning back to Derek. "She wants emotional satisfaction—not just fiscal—in her work."

Derek listened to the strains of a Christmas carol

being played a little farther down the hall. He wasn't sure why; he just knew the rendition of "Hark the Herald Angels Sing" made him feel melancholy. "What does Eve want in her personal life?" What could he have given her, and hadn't?

Her mother's expression gentled. "You really don't know?"

Desperate for help, he shook his head. "Apparently, I haven't got a clue," he remarked drily. Otherwise he would be with Eve right now, celebrating the best holiday of the year. Instead of flailing around, lost and at loose ends.

The older woman sent him another wry smile. "Then it's about time you found out, don't you think?"

"How?" Derek retorted in droll exasperation. "She won't talk to me!" Wouldn't answer his calls or his emails or his texts.

"Since when has that stopped you from going after what you want?" Marjorie asked, unimpressed. "You and I are a lot alike, you know. That's probably what attracts— and repels—Eve the most."

Reluctantly, Derek conceded that she had a point. He and Marjorie were both driven individuals.

"So, I know that if you really want to make something happen, you'll find a way." Marjorie paused meaningfully. "Same as me."

"WHAT DO YOU mean, you're not coming home?" Eve asked her mother on Christmas Eve morning. They always spent the holiday together, and Marjorie's release had already been scheduled.

"I decided to stay another couple of days."

Eve admired her mother's tenacity, even as she worried about her own lack of it. "Then I'll come to the cardiac rehab unit and spend it with you."

"No. I don't think that's a good idea."

Feeling more despondent than ever, Eve said, "You don't?"

Her mother continued brightly, "We can have dinner together in the dining room here on Christmas Day, and celebrate then."

"What about the rest of the time?" Eve demanded. There were over twenty-four hours between now and then! She had wanted a shoulder to lean on, an ear to listen. Comfort. And joy. And love. In short, all the things she could have had with Derek, if she'd only had the courage to take the leap of faith required, and see their relationship through.

"I'll be resting," her mother replied, as matter-of-fact as ever. "And you need the time to reflect, in any case."

Eve wasn't sure she wanted to do a lot of thinking about everything that had happened. Because thinking would lead to crying, and she had done enough of that. "You're sure?" she asked again, wishing she didn't already miss Derek—and Tiffany—so very much.

"Positive," her mother said, sounding positively cheerful and relaxed.

Feeling abandoned all over again, Eve sighed. "Okay...then, I'll see you tomorrow, Mom. And Merry Christmas."

"Merry Christmas to you, too, honey."

Eve hung up the phone.

A moment later, the doorbell rang.

She went to answer. On the porch in front of her condo was a wicker basket containing a DVD of *A Christmas Story,* a red-and-white-striped tin of popcorn and her favorite sparkling water. Attached to a box of peppermint bark, fastened with a big red bow, was a card that said, "You're right. We don't know as much about each other as I want to know. Maybe we should start by watching each other's favorite holiday movies. Derek."

What did that mean? Had he forgiven her? Was he ready to slow down and give her the space she had asked for?

And what was so great about spending Christmas Eve alone, anyway? Eve wondered grumpily. She knew from previous conversations with Derek that Tiffany was spending her evening with Craig and Carleen. Had Derek arranged to be with family, too? Or was he as alone—and miserable—as she was? About to sit down and watch her favorite holiday movie by himself?

There was only one way to find out!

DEREK HAD JUST turned on the DVD when his doorbell rang.

The melancholy sounds of *A Charlie Brown Christmas* filling his beautiful empty home, he went to see who was on the doorstep.

Eve stood there, looking like an angel from heaven. She was wearing a pretty red dress and a white wool coat. A silk scarf was looped around her neck, the gift basket he had left for her was by her side and two other presents were in her arms. With a hint of color in her sculpted cheeks, her golden-brown hair flowing over her shoulders, she looked as elegant and gorgeous as ever. "I hope I'm not intruding," she began.

If she only knew how much he'd been hoping she would reach out to him, the way he had been reaching out to her. Yet something in her eyes had him erring on the side of caution. Suppressing the impulse to wrap his arms around her and hold her close, he remained where he was and simply said, "You're not."

She flashed a brief smile. "I was out delivering thank-yous to clients and thought I'd stop by to give you this." She handed him a small gift-wrapped box bearing his name, and another with Tiffany's.

Was that it?

Just a business call?

He looked her in the eye, trying to decide.

"Merry Christmas," she said thickly.

Were those tears glistening in her amber eyes? Or was he just imagining the slight tremble of her lips?

She picked up the basket he'd left for her, and handed it to him, too.

"Merry Christmas to *you*." He set the gifts she'd brought him on top of the unopened ones he had left for her, in the basket.

Across the street, neighbors paused to observe.

Eve glanced over her shoulder, then turned back to him. "May I come in?" she asked quietly.

He narrowed his eyes, still trying to figure out what she was up to. Was this the ultimate kiss-off? Or something else entirely? Well, there was only one way to find out.

He nodded and stepped aside. She swept by him in a drift of hyacinth perfume.

Acknowledging that she had the power to break his heart all over again, he closed the door behind them, shutting the rest of the world out. At least for now.

Her head cocked at the distant sound of the *Peanuts* gang rehearsing a Christmas pageant. Derek led the way into the adjacent living area, where a beautifully decorated tree and more presents waited. The television was on. Snoopy and the gang were dancing uproariously, while Charlie Brown stood alone and looked on, exasperated, depressed and disillusioned.

"For the record, I haven't watched the movie yet," he said awkwardly. Although he had seen it before as a kid, many times.

As he set the basket down on the coffee table, he could see the seal on the DVD he'd given her was also intact. He figured whatever this was, they might as well get it over with. Particularly since she hadn't yet moved to take off her coat or scarf. He inclined his head at the gift basket. "You didn't like my gift?" Was she rejecting that, too?

"It was nice."

"But…?"

She lifted a shoulder. "It wasn't what I wanted, after all."

His heart, not to mention his pride, felt stomped on again.

"The being-apart-from-each-other bit," she amended hastily.

A muscle worked in his cheek. "What did you want?" he rasped.

Eve took a deep breath and came closer. "A do-over."

"A do-over?" he repeated dumbly.

She nodded. Took off her coat and then her scarf, and set both aside. Amber eyes locked with his, she came nearer still. Took both his hands in hers and squeezed lightly. She paused to look down at their entwined fingers. "I know I said I was upset because everything was happening too fast." She took another breath, then looked up again. "But I realize that wasn't it at all."

He followed his instincts and wrapped his arms around her. "Then what was it?"

She shrugged, looking tearful—and remorseful—

yet again. "It was that it was happening at all," she choked out. "I knew the first time we met that you had the power to change my world. It's why I found you so completely irritating."

Eve drew a breath and pushed on emotionally, "The first time we kissed, I knew you had the power to change my heart." She splayed her hands over his chest. "And the first time we made love, though I tried hard to deny it, it was pretty much a done deal."

Derek stroked his palm over her hair. "You rocked my world, too."

She nodded, truly accepting that in a way she never had before. Her voice dropped a notch. "The fact is, I've never wanted to be with anyone as much as I wanted to be with you, Derek. In truth, I didn't even know it was possible to love like this...."

With joy soaring through him, he pressed a finger to her lips. "Back up a minute," he demanded gruffly. "Did you say 'love'?"

Eve nodded, trembling all the more. "And not in the casual, maybe-we-should-consider-having-a-relationship kind of way, but the forever-and-ever kind." She swallowed hard, but her gaze didn't waver as she forged on. "And that scares the heck out of me, Derek, because I'm afraid something could or will happen, and we'll lose this—"

Knowing she wasn't the only one at fault here, Derek interrupted her. "For the record, what we feel for each other scares the heck out of me, too. Which is why I've been pushing so hard," he admitted hoarsely. "I wanted everything nailed down in a way that couldn't be undone. So it wouldn't be easy for us to walk away. When what I should have had all along was faith." He lifted her hand, kissed the back of it. "Faith in you, faith in me, faith in the two of us and the love we share. And in the life we could have, if we take the time to build a relationship that is strong enough to last through whatever fate throws our way."

Eve smiled, as at peace now as she was in love. "I do have faith in you, Derek."

"And I have faith in you." They kissed, sweetly and tenderly.

Finally, they drew apart.

Eve continued affectionately, "Enough confidence to want to not just pick up where we left off, but to take it to the next level."

She reached for the presents she'd brought him and had him open the first box, which contained a toy cradle for Tiffany's baby doll. In the second was an expensive gold watch with some simple words inscribed on the back: *No Time like the Present.*

Looking a little misty-eyed, he put the timepiece on and kissed her. "As long as we're getting gifts for each other…" Grinning mysteriously, he went to his desk, opened a drawer and returned with a jewelry box, which he handed her. It also contained a watch, with the inscription: *Slow and Steady Wins the Race.*

Eve laughed. "Great minds think alike."

Derek kissed her deeply. "They sure do. Now that we know time is on our side," he joked.

"And that we have all the time in the world," she added, laughing again.

They embraced, and kissed some more, even more poignantly. "So it's official? We're a couple?" Eve said.

Derek nodded. "For now and forever."

Epilogue

Christmas Eve, two years later...

"I really get to put the angel on top of the tree this year?" Tiffany asked.

"You sure do," Derek and Eve replied in unison. Eve handed her the angel. Derek lifted the three-year-old high enough to reach.

In a red tartan plaid dress, fitted red velvet vest, shimmery white tights and her favorite red cowgirl boots, her glossy brown curls swept into a bouncy ponytail, the little girl was beside herself with excitement.

As were they, Eve thought happily. She'd thought the same thing every year she had been with Derek, but she was sure this was going to be the best Christmas ever!

With his assistance, Tiffany settled the ornament on the top branch of the Fraser fir. With one arm laced about his broad shoulders, she leaned back against her daddy, wrinkling her nose and studying her handiwork.

Clearly possessing an artist's temperament, she asked finally, "What do you think?"

"It's perfect," Derek and Eve said simultaneously.

Tiffany giggled as Derek kissed the top of her head, then set her back down on the floor. She dashed over to accept a hug and kiss of congratulations from Eve, too.

"You two always say the same thing at the same time," the child declared, her blue eyes sparkling in delight.

Winking, Derek gathered both ladies close for a family hug. "That's because great minds think alike."

Eve laughed at the familiar refrain. Tiffany did, too, then wiggled out of the group hug. "I have to get the cookies for Santa!"

"The red dish with Santa's picture on it is on the table!" Eve called after her.

"'Kay!" Tiffany disappeared around the corner into the kitchen.

"So how are you doing?" Derek asked, putting a hand to Eve's tummy, where another little one, yet to be born, resided.

Basking in his solid warmth. Eve sighed in satisfaction. "I could not be happier. Which is," she teased, "a fact you well know."

He kissed her. "And a sentiment I share."

She and Derek had celebrated their one-year wedding anniversary the previous month, and found out shortly after that she was pregnant. Much to the entire family's delight, the baby would be born the following summer. Her mother had not only recovered fully from her heart attack, but gone on to win the top home sales award for Highland Park two years running. Marjorie had also found a new beau, Red Bloom, when the two realized they had more in common than a lust for business. And, Eve reflected with a smile, since buying and upgrading the ranch he had wanted in Laramie County as a weekend and holiday retreat, she and Derek saw a lot more of the McCabe clan, too.

Life, it had turned out, was pretty wonderful these days. And with the first of the children they had planned on the way, it only looked to get better. Smiling to herself, she watched as Tiffany glided back into the room, a half dozen of the cookies she had worked so hard on with Eve balanced precariously on the rimmed dish. "I think Santa's really going to like these," the little girl declared, setting them on a table near the sofas flanking the fireplace.

"I know he will," Derek and Eve said, once again speaking at the exact same time.

Tiffany erupted into a cascade of giggles that brought tears to their eyes. "You-all are so funny!" she exclaimed, then ran back to the kitchen to get the sippy cup of milk they'd already poured for Santa.

Derek took Eve into his arms. "Not to mention very much in love," she said softly, splaying her hands across his chest and kissing him tenderly.

"You've got that right," he murmured, kissing her back just as gently. He looked down at her, all the affection he felt reflected in his eyes. "Merry Christmas, Mrs. McCabe."

Eve wrapped her arms around him and hugged him close. She whispered sweetly, "Merry Christmas to you, too."

* * * * *

Watch for the next book in Cathy Gillen Thacker's
McCABE HOMECOMING *miniseries,*
THE TEXAS WILDCATTER'S BABY,
coming March 2014,
only from Harlequin American Romance!

Available January 7, 2014

#1481 HER CALLAHAN FAMILY MAN
Callahan Cowboys
Tina Leonard

When Jace Callahan and Sawyer Cash engaged in their secretive affair, neither of them anticipated an unplanned pregnancy. Jace wants to seal the deal with a quickie marriage...but it turns out he has a very reluctant bride!

#1482 MARRYING THE COWBOY
Blue Falls, Texas
Trish Milburn

When a tornado rips through Blue Falls, good friends Elissa Mason and Pete Kayne find themselves sharing a house. Suddenly Elissa is thinking about her *pal* in a whole new way....

#1483 THE SURPRISE HOLIDAY DAD
Safe Harbor Medical
Jacqueline Diamond

Adrienne Cavill delivers other women's babies, but can't have one of her own. Now she may lose the nephew she's raising, and her heart, to his long-absent father, Wade Hunter. Unless the two of them can come up with a different arrangement?

#1484 RANCHER AT RISK
Barbara White Daille

Ryan Molloy's job is running his boss's ranch, so he doesn't have time to babysit Lianne Ward. She's there to establish a boys' camp—and definitely doesn't need Ryan looking over her shoulder every minute!

———————

HARCNM1213

REQUEST YOUR FREE BOOKS!
2 FREE NOVELS PLUS 2 FREE GIFTS!

HARLEQUIN

American ★ Romance®

LOVE, HOME & HAPPINESS

YES! Please send me 2 FREE Harlequin® American Romance® novels and my 2 FREE gifts (gifts are worth about $10). After receiving them, if I don't wish to receive any more books, I can return the shipping statement marked "cancel." If I don't cancel, I will receive 4 brand-new novels every month and be billed just $4.74 per book in the U.S. or $5.24 per book in Canada. That's a savings of at least 14% off the cover price! It's quite a bargain! Shipping and handling is just 50¢ per book in the U.S. and 75¢ per book in Canada.* I understand that accepting the 2 free books and gifts places me under no obligation to buy anything. I can always return a shipment and cancel at any time. Even if I never buy another book, the two free books and gifts are mine to keep forever.

154/354 HDN F4YN

Name   (PLEASE PRINT)

Address   Apt. #

City   State/Prov.   Zip/Postal Code

Signature (if under 18, a parent or guardian must sign)

Mail to the **Harlequin® Reader Service:**
IN U.S.A.: P.O. Box 1867, Buffalo, NY 14240-1867
IN CANADA: P.O. Box 609, Fort Erie, Ontario L2A 5X3

Want to try two free books from another line?
Call 1-800-873-8635 or visit www.ReaderService.com.

* Terms and prices subject to change without notice. Prices do not include applicable taxes. Sales tax applicable in N.Y. Canadian residents will be charged applicable taxes. Offer not valid in Quebec. This offer is limited to one order per household. Not valid for current subscribers to Harlequin American Romance books. All orders subject to credit approval. Credit or debit balances in a customer's account(s) may be offset by any other outstanding balance owed by or to the customer. Please allow 4 to 6 weeks for delivery. Offer available while quantities last.

Your Privacy—The Harlequin® Reader Service is committed to protecting your privacy. Our Privacy Policy is available online at www.ReaderService.com or upon request from the Harlequin Reader Service.

We make a portion of our mailing list available to reputable third parties that offer products we believe may interest you. If you prefer that we not exchange your name with third parties, or if you wish to clarify or modify your communication preferences, please visit us at www.ReaderService.com/consumerschoice or write to us at Harlequin Reader Service Preference Service, P.O. Box 9062, Buffalo, NY 14269. Include your complete name and address.

HAR13R

*Their families may be rivals, but Jace Callahan
just can't stay away from Sawyer Cash!*

Jace Callahan appeared to be locked in place, thunderstruck. What had him completely poleaxed was that the little darling who had such spunk was quite clearly as pregnant as a busy bunny in spring.

She made no effort to hide it in a curve-hugging hot pink dress with long sleeves and a high waist. Taupe boots adorned her feet, and she looked sexy as a goddess, but for the glare she wore just for him.

A pregnant Sawyer Cash was a thorny issue, especially since she was the niece of their Rancho Diablo neighbor, Storm Cash. The Callahans didn't quite trust Storm, in spite of the fact that they'd hired Sawyer on to bodyguard the Callahan kinder.

But then Sawyer had simply vanished off the face of the earth, leaving only a note of resignation behind. No forwarding address, a slight that he'd known was directed at him.

Jace knew this because for the past year he and Sawyer had had "a thing," a secret they'd worked hard to keep completely concealed from everyone.

He'd missed sleeping with her these past many months she'd elected to vacate Rancho Diablo with no forwarding address. Standing here looking at her brought all the familiar desire back like a screaming banshee.

Yet clearly they had a problem. Best to face facts right up front. "Is that why you went away from Rancho Diablo?" he asked, pointing to her tummy.

She raised her chin. "It won't surprise me if you back out, Jace. You were never one for commitment."

Commitment, his boot. Of his six siblings, consisting of one sister and five brothers, he'd been the one who'd most longed to settle down.

He gazed at her stomach again, impressed by the righteous size to which she'd grown in the short months since he'd last seen her—and slept with her.

He wished he could drag her to his bed right now.

"I'm your prize, beautiful," he said with a grin. "No worries about that."

Look for HER CALLAHAN FAMILY MAN,
by USA TODAY bestselling author Tina Leonard
next month, from Harlequin® American Romance®.

American Romance®

Guess who's coming home
for Christmas…

Dr. Adrienne Cavill couldn't love her nephew more if
he were her own child. And no deadbeat dad is going to
claim the little boy she's practically raised.

Wade Hunter's past and future await the detective turned
P.I. He missed five years of his son's life, and nothing's
chasing him away this time. That includes the pretty
doctor who's giving his child everything—except the
father he needs.

Now that she knows the reasons why he left, how can
Adrienne keep the rugged ex-cop from his son—or from
her, for that matter? Will Christmas bring Adrienne the
family she never thought she could have?

The Surprise Holiday Dad
by JACQUELINE DIAMOND

Available January 2014,
from Harlequin® American Romance®.